Of Chickens and Hobos

Of Chickens and Hobos

B. LEANN JUENGERMAN
AUTHOR ACADEMY ELITE

This is a work of Historical Fiction. The characters and incidences in this story are real but have been altered to create a singular storyline. Any resemblance to persons living or dead is not coincidental. They are pretty much someone in my family as these are my family's stories. They were given to me by the main character, and other characters are purely imaginary.

Copyright 2020 by B. Leann Juengerman

All rights reserved. No part of this book may be used without written consent of the author except for book reviews and educational purposes.

First Edition, February 2020

Cover design by DaisyDesign

ISBN: 978-1-64085-997-5 (Paperback)
978-1-64085-998-2 (Hardback)
978-1-64085-999-9 (ebook)

Library of Congress Control Number: 2019917129

Published by Author Academy Elite, USA

*To the real
Elizabeth, Dale, and Denny*

Acknowledgements

It takes so many people to write a book. I was amazed at how many people were there to help. Thank you…

To family:

> My mom, Barbara Vines, for recognizing my passion for writing when I was in first grade
>
> Stormye Lin Rangel, for being brave enough to tell her aunt to rewrite the first chapter
>
> Tori, my step-mother, for agreeing with my mom and encouraging me as well
>
> My sister Martha and her husband Randy (aunt Martha and Uncle Randall) for support and help
>
> Ray Mullen for sharing your grandmother with me, and for believing in me enough to buy me my first computer

Franklin Beaver- for helping me through my classes in creative writing at SMU

Eric Juengerman- for believing in me enough to let me have my own office and time at Oxford, and the time you spent editing the final copy

Amber, Jackie, Joshua, and Keenen- for supporting a crazy mom with a crazy dream

To Roy Maynard, the first editor who assured me I would be published one day

To Robin Abess- for the hours and hours of reading, revision suggestions, and even a little bit of ghost writing in spots

To Anne Overman for hours of editing through several versions of this story

To all my teachers, but especially Miss Burt, Mrs. Cohen, and Mrs. Hornsby, my creative writing teacher

To my Oxford tutors, Jeremy Hughes and Jonathan Miles, and SMU Professor, Dr. Diane Betts

To Vanston Middle School staff and students from 2001-2017- Especially my fourth period class, who allowed me to use them as guinea pigs

To Bastrop Middle School Pre-AP students for helping me choose the cover art

To The DFW Writers Workshop- For helping me master my craft

To Kary Oberbrunner and the Authors Academy Elite team for your time and expertise

Mostly, to the real Elizabeth, Dale, and Uncle Denny, who gave me their stories to share.

Prologue

I can feel every eye in the courtroom on me. It's time.
Walking slowly to the front of the room, my hands tremble as I smooth out my new dress. My stomach is doing flip-flops that would make the Barnum and Bailey Circus proud.

Stopping in front of the chair by the judge, I place my hand on the scarred, leathered Bible that feels just like the one at my grandpap's farm. My other hand is still shaking as I raise it into the air to take the oath.

"State your name," says an older man in uniform.

"Elizabeth Anne Sundo."

"Do you swear to tell the truth, the whole truth, and nothing but the truth?" he asks.

"So help me God."

"You may take your seat."

I get settled and look at the people in the room. I hate being the center of attention, so having everyone stare at me is nerve-wracking. Setting my eyes on Mum is helping me calm my nerves a bit. She smiles encouragingly at me. Papa is sitting right next to her. He gives me one of those "You can do it!" signs that dads give. Having them in the courtroom makes me feel more secure; safe, just like when I was little and they would tuck me in bed at night.

Small beads of sweat begin to form the sides of my face, some of them tickling me as they roll down my cheeks. I swipe them away with the handkerchief Mum gave me, unsure if it's from the warm summer breezes coming in and out of the open windows or the quickening beats of my heart.

I will not look at "the defendant" at all, I've decided, but I will have to make eye contact with the lawyer walking over to me. There's no choice about that. At least he's nice. He'd told me beforehand what kind of questions he would be asking; questions like how did we know about the fake names? When did we suspect about the money? Why was I in the office at three in the morning? And how did Dale and Tommy just happen to know where I was?

I am to tell the story from the beginning. Technically, that would be impossible. I could say it was when we started referring to the economy as a Great Depression. Perhaps it could be the day Papa's boss came to him and told him he didn't have a job anymore. Maybe it was the night of my parents' big argument. For that matter, I could've blamed it on Aunt Martha because she was the one who had brought the apple butter over to our house the day Dale left. But mostly, I think it was the day Mum came home with her "Great News."

Without meaning to, I grit my teeth hard, holding back some tears. It doesn't matter where the beginning was. The ending is still the same, and there's nothing I can do about it.

CHAPTER ONE

"Great" News

Mr. Bedgood, my English teacher, once told me I "needed to find my voice" when I write. I had no idea what he meant, so I asked him. He said it meant I needed to find my own unique style, to show off my personality and my attitude. I wasn't sure I could do that. It was hard enough speaking up for myself out loud, much less on paper, but I told him I'd work on it.

I've always wanted to be a writer, like Louisa May Alcott or Lucy Maud Montgomery. I've even had ideas of becoming a female reporter someday, even though it's a job mostly for men. I want to go to college, see the world, and write books and newspaper articles. That's what I want in life, but I don't know if that's what I'm going to get.

Especially after the day Mum came home with her "Great News."

I was working on homework when she came through the front door, and for once, she was in a wonderful mood. It had been a while since I'd seen her happy. She'd been depressed since the day we woke up and found my brother, Dale, had run away from home in the middle of the night. I know he left us to find work, but a fat lot of good that did. Yes, for him, it was great. It meant he was free and could work wherever he wanted. For me though, it meant staying home with two distraught parents, watching them cry, and getting ignored. For several weeks, every conversation in the house was about Dale, money, or the economy. I was non-existent. It's hard to "find your voice" when you aren't even heard in your own home.

"I've got some great news fer ya!" she happily announced to Papa and me, her faint Irish accent coming out in her speech.

"Did you get a letter from Dale?" I squealed.

Her entire demeanor changed. I was met with a cold stare and a very curt, "No."

That's about normal. He leaves home, and I get griped at. I got quiet.

The silence was awkward, so Papa broke it with, "So what's this great news then?"

Mum's smile returned, even though it wasn't as happy as it had been. "There are some job openings down to the factory, and they're takin' young people. I've already secured a place for ya at work. Isn't that wonderful?"

"You found me some work?" Papa asked.

"No, silly," she said. "I've got a job fer Beth!"

"Me?"

"Yes!"

Great news? Uhm, *no.*

Not me. I wanted to stay in school. I wanted to write. I didn't want to go to work, especially at that factory. Mum had been working at the Hillerman Chicken Factory for a little over a year, since the day Papa lost his job. I know what she did. She stood all day long, cutting up chickens to be canned.

How many times have I heard her complain about the way she and the other workers were treated? She'd told us how they hired mostly women so they wouldn't have to pay as much, and immigrants got paid even less. Mum still had her Irish accent, so that meant she was one of the "foreigners." She'd told tons of stories about how mean the boss man was, how dirty they kept the floors, and how long her hours were.

But now, suddenly, it's great?

"And ya can make up ta a dollar a week!"

Uhm, twenty cents a day? Seriously?

I stood there, stunned, with both of my parents staring at me. I couldn't speak at first because I was afraid of whatever would come out of my mouth. I guess the silence was all right with my folks because Mum chatted happily on and on about it.

"It's a great opportunity, and ya won't be far away from me, and the money t'would help us out."

My first thought was to be diplomatic about it. So, I lied.

"I appreciate it, Mum," I said with all the enthusiasm I could muster, "but I think I should stay at school because I want to become a nurse someday."

I didn't really, but being a nurse sounded more honorable and more likely than becoming a writer, and I thought she'd be proud of me for choosing to have a career. I also hoped she'd like the idea of me doing a job where I could help people.

She didn't budge. "Elizabeth, we can use the money. And ya can start tomorrow."

"Tomorrow! But-" I practically screamed, but by then she was already on her way into the kitchen. I could feel my eyes filling with tears and my breath getting caught in my throat as I attempted to push down the sobbing inside me.

No last day of school? No telling my friends goodbye? No Allison? No Tommy? No saying goodbye to my teachers? Why?

And I wasn't lying about staying in school. I wanted to be where my friends were. My mind kept running through memories of socials and recesses and doing homework together. We even had enough girls to get our first girls' basketball team this year, and I wanted to be on it. It felt like everything I loved about my life was being taken away from me.

How on Earth could she think this was "great news?"

But there wasn't much I could say. Children were still to be seen and not heard.

I looked imploringly at Papa. When he told me to wait for them in the living room, I didn't argue. Surely he would talk some sense into her, I thought, and I wouldn't have to go to work.

But after a twenty-minute discussion behind closed doors, he seemed to be for it, too. I knew right then that I would never become a writer, or a nurse, or a basketball player. I would become a worker in a chicken factory.

By the time Mum came to get me out of bed the next morning, I was already awake. It's hard to sleep when you are waking up every few hours with words ringing in your ears. "We really need the money. You can make up ta a dollar a week! Isn't that wonderful?"

When she came in, I rolled over to face the wall. I didn't want her to know I was already awake. When she told me to get up, I rolled back over and just glared at her before getting out of bed and stomping over to the closet to look for something to wear.

She left quietly. I grabbed one of the dresses from my closet and stomped just as hard as I could back to my bed. If they didn't know for sure how angry I was, I was darned well going to make sure they found out.

So I clomped to the bathroom to brush my teeth, I trudged back to my room to braid my hair, and I treaded over to my dresser for a piece of string to tie off my braid. I hoped they had heard every bit of it downstairs.

Maybe, I hoped silently, they would realize this was a bad idea, and when I got there, they'd say it was ok and say

I didn't have to go. So I marched down the stairs making as much noise as I could and came to the door of the kitchen. I stood in icy silence, waiting.

Instead, they were carrying on as if I'd never existed. Mum was sipping tea at the table, and Papa was eating a biscuit and looking through a newspaper. They were discussing some job postings in the "wanted" section.

"And they'll need several men for that. It also says this could lead to a full-time job."

Seriously? Did they not hear all the ruckus upstairs?

"That t'would be lovely," Mum was saying.

Nope. Nothing. My wish was definitely not going to come true.

I groaned and went to the counter by the sink and grabbed some biscuits. I began slicing into each one and putting apple butter or jam onto them.

Papa was saying, "If that were to happen, I could get the permanent position, and we could let Beth go back to school."

I rolled my eyes and muttered a quiet, "Why bother?"

Maybe I shouldn't have said that, I know. The thought of Papa finding work should've made me happy, but I also knew better than to get my hopes up. The last time Papa went for a job interview, there were over a hundred men trying to get three positions. Papa had waited all day in the heat for nothing.

But me, lucky me, I got to go to work and never had to have an interview at all!

My eyes welled up again. The biscuit was warm in my hand, but I was too near to tears to eat it. Just as well that I didn't because Mum announced it was time to leave. I wrapped the warm biscuits in a cloth and stuffed them into my pocket. Mum handed me a lunch pail and my coat, then we headed out the door to begin our long walk to the factory.

Once we were outside, in the darkness, we didn't speak. I was afraid she was going to try explaining to me again what a great thing this job was, or worse, try to get me to talk to her.

Thankfully, she didn't. But just in case, I stuffed a bite of the biscuit in my mouth.

The warm biscuit was delightful, and I was enjoying it until I started noticing the houses we were passing on our way into Pittsburgh. Almost every one of them was dark and quiet; only a few had a light or two on. Most likely, the families inside were enjoying blissful sleep while we were out in the very cool air. Soon, everyone would be waking up, and the kids would all start getting ready for school.

Suddenly, the biscuit was like clay in my mouth. My breathing started to speed up and I could feel myself holding back tears again. It hit me that I wouldn't be at school. No friends, no gossiping, no giggling, no trying to see Tommy in the hallways.

That also meant there would be no college, no writing, and no traveling.

The anger and tears just started flowing. My hands were shaking, and I had to do something to feel like I was fighting back. In a time when wasting food is not an option, I did the most defiant thing I could. When Mum wasn't looking, I threw down the rest of my biscuit even though it only had one bite taken out of it. I didn't care if it was wasteful; I wasn't going to eat it.

There was still a silence as we walked. Then I started seeing more and more people. Some smiled and waved, others walked too quickly to notice us. One or two said hi to Mum just as we turned the corner, and that's when I saw the factory for the first time.

A strange feeling of panic started to engulf me as we walked past the large, wrought-iron fence. Hundreds of people were forming two lines near the front gates. I started to walk up to the first line we came to, but I noticed Mum kept going. "Come along, Beth," she said.

No matter how mad you get at your parents, there are times you just want to be near them. When she called me to her, I scurried over as quickly as I could.

I looked around, almost gawking at all the people. I'm not the most outgoing person around, and the thought of so many people was overwhelming. As I stood next to her, shivering, I started looking into the two lines. Both lines were filled with mostly women and a few men, but there was something different about the other line. Something seemed to be a little off. After a few moments, my curiosity grew stronger than my anger, and I just had to say something.

"Mum, what are these two lines for?"

She looked around like she had never noticed it before. "Oh, this line is fer those who already have jobs, and the other is fer those lookin' fer work."

That's when I realized why the two columns were so different. In our line, people were quite chatty; greeting each other, joking around, talking and gossiping. The other row was silent; desperate. Dozens of women stood, shivering in thin cotton dresses and sweaters, willing to take even one day's worth of work.

Then my heart jumped, like it forgot to beat for a minute. Waiting in the other line was our former neighbor, Mrs. Fitzgerald. I say former neighbor because she doesn't live at her house anymore. She lives in her car.

Life is so unfair sometimes. Here were all these women waiting for interviews, hoping for work so they could feed their families, and here I was, only 14 and going to work when I desperately wanted to be back in school. Turning my back toward them, I couldn't help but feel like I was taking something from them.

At six o'clock sharp, a shrill whistle blew at the gates, causing me to jump. Two large men in overalls appeared out of nowhere and pushed open the iron gates. I followed Mum into the factory to begin my first day of work.

For a minute there, I honestly thought I was going to throw up.

CHAPTER TWO
The First Day

Once those gates opened, people scattered into the plant like ants on a giant piece of cake. I'm only four-foot-ten, and I don't think I've ever realized until that day just how short I am. So many people were wandering around, and there were only one or two shorter than me. I walked quickly, zig-zagging between them, trying desperately to stay out of their way and still follow Mum into the building.

The inside of the factory was even more depressing than the outside. The hallways were dark, the walls bare, and—just as Mum had said—the floors were dirty.

Inside, I was hurting bad, but I couldn't let anyone see it. People can be mean if they think you're weak. I guess it gives them some kind of feeling of power. Like this girl at school, Sadie. She's that type. A couple of years ago I found a book on a library table with *Sadie Moore* clearly written in it. I knew who she was because she was in Dale's class, so I thought I'd be nice and take it to her. But that girl is beyond mean. Instead of getting a "thank you," or even a "kiss my foot," she yanked it out of my hands before I could say anything. She started screaming at me in front of the entire school, yelling about how I stole it from her. Then the teachers got involved and I had to stay an extra thirty minutes after school, getting lectured on not touching what wasn't mine.

Even after the teachers found out she'd lied, nothing happened to her. I think it's because her father works at a bank and no one wants to upset people with money. It's not fair, but that's how it seems to be.

Mum and I made our way down a hallway, away from the chaos and toward the quieter rooms beside the loading docks. She entered one of the small offices to the left and took a seat. I paused at the door, looking into the almost empty room, but she motioned for me to stand behind her. Inside, there was a desk, some chairs, and some filing cabinets. Except for the large mantle clock on the filing cabinet and a nasty-looking girly calendar on the wall, there was nothing else to the room. It looked like a dungeon, waiting for the dragon to enter.

Then Mr. Reed came in.

I didn't know his name at the time, but that's who he was. He was a large man with sizable sweat stains on his white shirt, and his suspenders were worn from years of holding his pants around his rotund middle. There was a saying that fat people were jolly, but there was no laughter or kindness in this man's eyes. None. He stood staring at me for a moment, and I noticed his eyes slowly going up and down my body. I trembled.

"Is this her?" he growled at Mum.

"Aye-yah," she said, which was her way of saying yes. "This is me daughter, Elizabeth."

He looked me up and down again, making me feel like a piece of meat in the butcher shop. I just stared down at my shoes.

"She's awful scrawny for 15," he growled as he walked over and took a seat behind his desk. I started to correct him and tell him I was only 14, and I only look younger than that because I'm so short, but Mum talked before I did.

"She's 15, I can assure ya of that."

I sucked in my breath. I'd never heard my mum lie in all my life. I tried not to show surprise, but my eyes went wide; I know it.

"All right," he huffed. "Put her at the vats with Anna."

"Yes, sir," Mum said as she stood. We left without another word. I followed her into the work area. It was a fairly dark area, filled with conveyor belts, boxes, vats, and push carts stuffed with chickens. Walking past some tables, we came to some huge, round vats of water. My eyes were busy taking in the size of the place, so at first I didn't notice the girl standing there.

"Good mornin', Anna," Mum said to the girl.

"Good mornin', Mrs. Sundo," she replied.

"Anna, this is me daughter, Elizabeth. Beth, this is Anna."

Anna turned and gave a welcoming smile, and I knew immediately I liked her. I really thought I'd be stuck with some older woman constantly telling me what to do. This girl, on the other hand, was about my age and only a little taller than me. She was wearing a sort of raincoat and firemen's boots. Then I realized her hair was braided down her back, just like mine, except her hair was red and mine is dark brown.

"That'll be lovely!" Anna chirped. "I could stand ta have some friends 'round here."

Mum smiled and said, "I'm leaving ya in good hands, m' dear. Have a good day and I'll see ya at lunchtime." She waved and began moving away.

"Mum!" I called after her. My voice began shaking again because I was struggling to keep from crying. I didn't care how nice Anna was, I still panicked when I saw my mum walking away. "Where will you be?"

"I'll be just over a short distance from ya, cutting the chickens," she said, and walked on to her station. Nervously, I turned to Anna, standing there like a big lump, but she quickly took charge.

"First, Elizabeth, let's get ya a coat an' some boots," she said, walking over to a line of lockers. "Ya'll be wantin' ta wear those ta kape from gettin' blood all o'er yer clothes, an' ya kin put yer lunch pail in this locker."

I smiled a little at her accent. It was just like Mum's, only much thicker.

"Please," I told her, "call me Beth. I don't go by Elizabeth." Then I giggled and added, "Unless I'm in trouble."

"All right then, Beth," she said with a smile. "That'll do. Now, put yer lunch there and grab a coat. They're o'er here, the jackets are. These chickens can ruin a dress, ya know, so ya should put one on the first thing every mornin'." She reached into a closet and pulled out a jacket and boots just like hers. I slipped the jacket on, but Anna had to help me with the boots, which were much too big on me.

I clunked around in the boots for a minute, trying to get the feel of them. Then we headed back to the vats.

"So, how old are ya?" she asked.

I tensed up. What was I supposed to say—15 or 14? I looked around desperately, like a spy making sure they weren't surrounded by the enemy. Then I whispered, as much as you can whisper in a large workroom, "I'm 14. But my mum told that big man I was 15. I mean, I will be 15 in November, but still…"

Then I got nervous, thinking I had said too much. "You aren't gonna tell on me, are you?"

Anna just laughed. "That man's the main boss down here. Name's Mr. Reed, an' I can tell ya why yer mum lied. He probably knows yer real age, and he figures if he kin hire children, he kin skimp on the pay."

I realized that's what my mum had said, too, about him wanting to keep the pay costs down to a minimum. She was just not as blunt about it.

Anna continued. "This way, he kin say ta his boss that someone else lied ta him about yer age so he can'nat get in trouble fer it, what with these new laws about child labor. He's jest trying to save his own hide. I've always wondered if he's gettin' any money back from the way he's cheatin' people. I would'nat doubt it." She glared into the direction of the offices.

What a relief. She wouldn't tell and here I'd been worried I'd get in trouble on the first day.

Then, for a brief, shimmering moment, I thought that might just be my ticket back to school. If I were to let on about how old I was, perhaps I'd be fired!

Yet in that next moment, I realized Mum might find me an even worse job if this didn't work out. I sighed, realizing my best option was to keep quiet and pretend to be 15.

As we neared the vats, I saw a big cart full of chickens and an empty cart next to it. Anna began her lessons.

"Tisn't really that difficult," she said with a bit of a sigh. "Take one o' the chickens, then a scrub brush like this, an' just clean it off. Ya must make sure that ya get rid o' all the feathers an' dirt. Then ya put it on the other cart, an' when 'tis full, we'll be takin' it ta yer Mum an' her friends ta be cut before cannin'. Then we'll go get another cart."

I knew how to cook, and I'd cleaned many a chicken before, so I didn't hesitate to grab one and plunge it into the water, but I yanked my hands back out with a yelp.

"Yikes! That's freezing!"

"Aye-yah," she said with a chuckle. "I was tryin' ta warn ya, but ya were too quick fer me."

I looked at her like I couldn't trust her, but I knew that was silly. She was right. I went charging in without letting her finish, so it was my own fault.

"Sorry about that, but it does warm up as ya continue werking," she told me.

Dipping my hands back into the icy water again, I retrieved the abandoned chicken. I grabbed the brush and started scrubbing with all my might. The water was so cold I thought it'd never warm up. Finally, I lifted the meat to be examined, glad to have my hands out of the water for even a moment.

"Pretty good," she told me, "But see here? Look at the skin beneath the wing. This hides dirt an' ya must clean that as well."

Looking closely, I could see what she was talking about, even though it wasn't much. I dipped in again, scrubbing that small area, looking for more hiding spots. With one last rinse, she was satisfied. I placed the chicken carefully on the cart. Anna tossed one onto the cart, grabbed another and was halfway finished with it before I could really get started again. Boy, she was quick.

As I grabbed another chicken, I had a thought. "So, how old are you?"

"Seventeen," she told me. "Started workin' here meself when I just came o'er from Ireland, an' we-"

"Miss Scott," a voice said from behind her. We turned and saw a woman standing near the vats. She was heavy and statuesque; the epitome of elegance. With her tweed skirt and matching business jacket, she seemed out of place in the grimy factory. Her subtle movements, her silky voice, it was as if we were peasants and the queen had just graced us with her presence. I stood up straight, like I was about to meet royalty.

"Miss Scott, is this Mrs. Sundo's daughter?"

"Aye-yah," Anna said with her bright smile, "Mrs. Fredericks, this is Beth."

The woman looked me over like she was sizing me up. I stood, hoping to make a good impression. There was a deep breath, then she started what sounded like a speech she had rehearsed and presented many times before.

"Welcome, Beth. I am Mrs. Fredericks. I am the line boss in your area. At the Hillerman Chicken Factory, we are a family, and as such, we all work hard for the good of our family. You could even think of me as your older sister, here to help if you find that you are in need of assistance. If you need anything, Anna can show you my office, and you may come to me with your problems or concerns any time."

"Thank you," we both replied.

"Good day, girls," she said with a small smile, then she walked over to another cutting table and began to talk to someone else. There was something so graceful about her that I admired.

"She seems quite pleasant," I told Anna.

"Maybe she is," Anna leaned in to tell me, "but don't be talkin' ta her unless ya'd like the entire plant knowin' yer business."

Alarmed, I leaned over to hear her more clearly. "You mean she's a blabbermouth? But, but she seems so, I don't know… refined." It was the only word I could think of.

"Aye-yah, she's a mean one. Best ta make sure ya stay on 'er good side. And don't be tellin' any stories ta her. She'd have Reed knowing everythin' a'fore the end o' the day."

It amazes me how some people can look like they have so much class on the outside but apparently not on the inside. I watched as she walked over to another one of the cutting tables and began talking with a group of ladies. How could someone who looked so pleasant be like that?

We turned back to our work, and I noticed a large clock on one of the walls near the lockers. The hands on it reminded me I only had eleven and a half hours left, for which I would make twenty whole cents.

CHAPTER THREE
Lunch with Anna (and Harold)

The morning seemed to take forever, but it would have been much worse if I hadn't had Anna to talk to. She was funny, quick witted, and full of good stories. We scrubbed, talked and laughed all morning. She gave me all kinds of advice, things like how to get more work done, who to talk to and who to avoid, and how to take care of my arms at night.

"Before ya go ta bed tonight, make sure ya put petroleum jelly on yer arms and hands. Then wrap 'em with some socks ta kape them moist. If ya don't, ye'll be havin' some pain, I kin tell ya that fer sure."

"Really?" I was surprised. "Why?"

"Tis the cold water. It'll make yer skin too dry."

I took mental notes and decided to tell Mum about that on the way home. Well, I'd tell her if we were speaking yet. After all, I still wasn't very happy.

Overhead, a shrill whistle blew.

"That'll be lunch," she said, grabbing the carts of chicken and pushing them toward the giant coolers in the back. She and several others slid their carts into the large cooler so they could continue working after lunch. Then she came back and told me to follow her.

"Let's store our jackets, but leave yer boots on. They're too hard ta put back on when lunch is over."

I placed my jacket in my locker and grabbed my lunch pail. Anna only took out a blanket from hers.

"Let's go outside!" she said. "It should be nice ta be out of the plant."

"Are we allowed to do that?" I asked, wanting to make sure I didn't get into trouble on my first day.

"Of course," she said. "Let's go tell yer mum where we'll be so she'll not worry."

I followed her to Mum's locker to let her know where we were going, then we went out the side doors. It was glorious. The chill from the morning was gone, and so were the lines of people. I wondered how many of them got jobs.

Once we were out on the grounds of the factory, Anna laid down the blanket as a place for us to sit. As soon as I got settled, I pulled out the small lunch Mum had made for me and began to munch on an apple.

"Anna, how many people do you think they hired this morning?"

She was smoothing out the blanket, getting rid of as many wrinkles as she could. "Don't know. Tis hard ta say. I doubt 'twas very many. 'Tis sad, really, the way the economy is going. They say in the papers this depression is gettin' better, but I'm not so sure."

I thought again about Mrs. Fitzgerald, waiting in line for a job. She'd had such a hard life since the stock market crashed. First, her husband lost his job and decided to leave the family to search for work. That was three or four years ago, and no one had heard from him since. Some people say he died, and some say he ran off with another woman. Either way, she was left on her own. Then she lost her house and had to send her three kids out west to be adopted by families who could afford to feed them. After that, she began living in her car.

I can't imagine a more horrid life. I wished with all my might that she got the job.

"Hey!" I said to Anna, who had leaned back on the blanket to rest her eyes, "Aren't you eating?"

"Uhm, nay," she said. "I try ta wait until I get home. Me family does'nat really have enough fer three meals a day, e'en with me pay. So I just eat breakfast an' dinner."

I felt a pang in my stomach. I sat for a minute, realizing I'd been petty and thrown out part of my breakfast. Then I remembered the biscuits in my pocket and pulled them out.

"Why don't you take some of my biscuits?" I asked. "I have them left over from breakfast and I still have an apple and a sandwich for lunch. I'll never eat all of it."

Anna sat up and stared at me curiously. "I'm ok. Really."

"But Anna, if Mum finds out I didn't eat these, she'll fuss at me for being wasteful. Please take some of these biscuits."

I doubt Mum would've really noticed, but it worked. Slowly, she reached for one.

"All right," she said, "but just ta help ya out. I can'nat be takin' charity."

"It isn't charity; it's avoiding waste. Mum's always trying to fatten me up, and I can't eat all of this."

Gingerly, she bit into the biscuit, and even with the dried out preserves on them, I could see on her face that she enjoyed every bite. I added another item to the mental notes I'd been taking all morning: *bring extra biscuits whenever possible.*

After we ate, we sat back on her blanket and enjoyed the sun on our faces on an unusually warm spring day. We were talking quietly when I heard a strange man's voice behind us.

"What are you girls whispering about?" I jumped a bit and turned to see a young man taking a seat on the blanket behind us. He was probably only two or three years older than me, yet his pudgy appearance and thick black glasses made him look much older.

"Ay, go away, Harold," Anna said, and I immediately recognized the name. She had warned me about Harold earlier. He was on the "Who to Avoid" list. She'd told me he was a brown-noser of the worst sort, hitting on every new girl at the plant and thinking he was such a catch. In reality, he was just a flat tire—disappointing and not too bright.

I looked at him. Too bad he was such a jerk and liked to suck-up to the bosses, because he sure had beautiful green eyes under those thick glasses.

"I'm just here to introduce myself to the new girl," he said, sticking out his hand for me to shake. "Hello, my name's Harold."

I went ahead and shook his hand, just to be polite. "Beth Sundo."

"Charmed," he said. "So how long have you been working here? You must be new, because I know I would have remembered seeing you before."

Yep. Just as Anna said.

"Aye-yah, this is my first day."

"Ah, well, that explains it. I know where all of the pretty girls work in this factory. Perhaps I need to come by and see you more often. Do you work with Anna? At the cleaning vats?"

"Aye-yah, she does," Anna answered for me, "An' if I see ya around our werk area, I'll pour water on ya!"

"Gadzooks! I do believe you're jealous," he said with a mean gleam in his eye.

Oh, boy, this guy was everything she told me he was.

"Ha! Jealous? Are ya kiddin' me? If anythin' I'll be feelin' sorry fer her. Go away."

"What did I do?" he asked with a pretend innocence.

"Nothin' in particular," she quipped, "except fer yer bein' a pest as usual."

Harold began to ignore her altogether. "So, Beth, how are you liking the job? I bet it's a lot better than being at school, eh?"

"Actually, no," I said as curtly as I could. I might not be good at speaking my mind like Anna, but I didn't have to be nice, that's for sure.

"Ah, well, I'm sorry to hear that. Maybe I need to come visit you sometime and keep you company; perhaps when she's not around?" he said, nodding in Anna's direction.

It didn't bother me at all when Anna ignored him and stood up to fold her blanket. I rose as well, and straightened my dress, taking off the sweater I'd been wearing all morning. I stretched my arms and legs.

"We'll be needin' ta hurry," Anna said. "The whistle will be soundin' soon."

"All right," I agreed. "It was nice meeting you, Harold." It was then that I noticed he was rather short and couldn't help but chuckle inside my head.

"I thought it was nice meeting you as well," he said with a smile. "So, I would like to accompany you to your work area, if you don't mind."

"T'isn't necessary," Anna said sharply. "We're big girls. We can find it ourselves." Of course, he wouldn't take the hint. Ugh.

"Oh, but I wouldn't dream of letting two such lovely ladies walk alone," he continued.

There just seemed to be no getting rid of this boy. Maybe he had nice eyes and looked harmless, but he made me feel very uncomfortable. Unfortunately, since we were all heading the same direction, we didn't have much of an alternative except to let him walk with us.

We kept silent, letting Harold chatter on as we made our way back to the building. We had just entered the building when I heard the most terrifying sound.

CHAPTER FOUR

Day's End

"Miss Sundo!" A big booming voice was calling my name. I turned and saw the man from earlier in the day, Mr. Reed, charging toward me like a freight train. His eyes were wide, his face red with anger.

We'd only met once, so I had no idea what I could have done for this man to be so upset with me.

"When you put the chickens in the refrigeration area, you left the door open, you stupid ninny!"

I gasped; the tears started again. There was no way I could stop them.

"Do you know how much money we've lost because of your dumb mistake?!" he continued. "How could you be such an idiot?"

"But, I-" was all I got out of my mouth. That's when Anna came to my rescue.

"Ya can'nat be yellin' at her like that! She wasn't anywhere near the refrigeration area, ya big eejit!"

Anna calling him the Irish word for idiot just added to his fury. "It was wide open, and I'm docking everyone's pay to make up for the losses!"

"But Mr. Reed!" I tried to speak but never got a chance.

"She doesn't even know where tha cold room is!" Anna was still going. She was almost right up in his face, and I stood there with my mouth going up and down like a dying fish.

He raised his fist to backhand her but suddenly stopped. I guess it was because people surrounding us would have seen. I hadn't even realized how many folks had were in the area, watching. Everyone was silent, eyes wide with fear and curiosity.

With a grunt, he lowered his hand and walked off.

My hands were shaking by this point. Everyone else left, and I noticed Harold was nowhere in the vicinity.

Mum came running up to us, fear all over her face.

"What on earth is going on?"

"Mum, I'm so sorry!" That's all I could manage, and I fell into her arms in tears.

Anna walked over and put an arm over my shoulders. "Reed's on one of his terrors, an' dockin' our pay for somethin' I know yer daughter did'nat do."

"Well what did he say?"

"Aw, he says she left the refrigerator door open, an' tha chicken is bad now, but I know 'tis not the truth he's tellin'. She was'nat even near the door. I took the chicken there meself."

Mum looked at her and then at me, and back to her. "Well, could you be the one who left it open?"

"No, ma'am," she said. "I know 'twas closed, because it caught me jacket on the way out, an' I had ta close it again. That's why I remember."

Mum sighed. "I was afraid of that. Don't ya be worrying about it, Beth. There's nothing ta be done except ta stay on his good side. When he calms down, I'm sure Mrs. Fredericks can talk some sense into him."

"Well, good luck with tha' one," Anna said as we started to walk off. "I'll be takin' yer daughter with me an' get back ta werk."

"Thank you, Anna," Mum said. She hugged me and told me she'd meet me at the front doors after work so we could walk home together, then she went off in hopes of finding Mrs. Fredericks. As we walked back, I was still holding off tears.

I know that, at times, it seems like I am the world's biggest cry-baby, but during those first few days, I couldn't help it. First, I get told I have to get a job I don't want, but then when I do get the job, I get yelled at for doing it wrong!

Anna went to retrieve the chickens from the refrigeration area while I got back into my jacket. As she walked off, I watched her, thinking about how she'd handled Mr. Reed. She wasn't afraid of him. Really, she didn't seem to be afraid of anything.

Me, on the other hand, I'm afraid of pretty much everything. I never took up for myself when kids at school teased me, I couldn't stand up to my parents, and now I couldn't talk to Mr. Reed. My English teacher had been right. I had to find my voice, and not just in my writing.

When she returned, Anna was storming mad; worse than when Reed was yelling at us. She chunked one of the chickens into the vat, slinging water everywhere.

"What's wrong?"

"Oh, that man! Here he's been tellin' us we've ruined the chickens, but when I go in there, nothin's ruined. Not one single piece of chicken has been thrown out."

I stared at her. "So?"

"So, he's lyin' ta ya about the doors. They definitely were'nat open."

"Why would he lie?"

"I can'nat prove it, but I think he's been takin' money from our paychecks."

I was wide-eyed. "What are you going to do? Should we tell Mum about it?"

"No," she waved it off and started back to work. "I'm just a kid meself. No one's gonna listen ta me, especially over a coin here an' a coin thare. But I'll kape watchin' him, and when I find the evidence, I'll be takin' him ta task. He'll be sorry then."

The walk home with Mum was almost as quiet as it had been in the morning, but not because I was still mad. Frankly, I think I was too tired to be angry. Plus, I was relieved to find out that Mum had talked Mrs. Fredericks into only docking our pay by a few cents, and I didn't want to think about the entire incident.

The fading sun was warm, and the layers of purples and pinks across the sky were beautiful. It gave me a moment of peace and hope. There was no need to spoil the walk with words.

Papa greeted us as soon as we entered the door. "How's my working girl?" he asked.

I couldn't look him in the eye, and my voice shook as I said, "Fine."

"Just fine?" he pressed.

"Uhm, yes." I was starting to get angry again.

Seriously? What was he wanting to hear? That I'd had so much fun I didn't want to go back to school? That I was ok with him and Mum making me go somewhere with a mean boss and water that was so cold I needed to wrap my hands?

So I just talked about one thing I could report. "There is this really nice girl named Anna. She's showing me how to do my job, and she let me know who the good eggs around the plant are and who to keep away from. Other than that, there's nothing to talk about. I clean chickens."

We stood in silence for a moment, then he smiled. "Well, my darling, I think I have some good news that might cheer you up."

"Really?" I squealed with a sudden burst of energy. "What is it?"

"Oh, no," he teased. "Not until dinner."

"Oh, Papa, please!" I begged, but he just went back to the kitchen to finish cooking dinner.

I hoped he was going to tell me he'd found a job and I could go back to school. That would be *so* nice.

He wouldn't tell me, so I did everything I could to help speed up dinner. I set the table, washed off the soup spoon, and got the glasses filled with water.

Finally, we sat down to eat. I couldn't eat because I was so excited.

"Ok, Papa! Now will you tell me?"

"Tell ya what?" Mum asked. I had forgotten that she had gone upstairs the minute we got home, so she didn't know about his secret news.

"Well," Papa said, "I told Beth I have some good news and some bad news."

"Wait, you never mentioned bad news."

He frowned. "Well, the bad news is that I didn't get that job working for the city. There were two openings and about fifty men there. I'm sorry, Margaret. I tried."

What? He didn't get a job?

All my enthusiasm was gone. Mum just put her hands on his and said, "I know, honey. I'm sorry, too. So now then, what's the good news?"

Papa's face brightened. "We got a letter from Dale!"

Mum and I screamed, asking question after question. He handed the letter to Mum. "He's in Oklahoma, working for the Civilian Conservation Corps."

Mum read the letter out loud, and it was short, but it let us know that he was safe, and he was working. That was the first time in a long time that Mum chatted so happily during dinner.

And just like that, I was invisible again.

She talked only to Papa. I couldn't get a word in edgewise.

When we finished, Mum left to go share the letter with Aunt Martha, who lived just a short ride away by bus. Papa looked at me and said, "Why don't you go on up to your room and let me do the dishes?"

"Oh, Papa, I can't let you do that," I said. "You did all the cooking."

"You've been working all day, Love, so let me work now."

I smiled. "All right, I can let you if you really want to."

"I do," he said, so I kissed him on the cheek and went to my room to read. I was thinking about putting the petroleum jelly on my arms as I sat down on my bed to take off my shoes. However, the bed was so inviting that I decided to lay down for a few minutes. Before I knew it, my arms were aching and Mum was saying, "Beth, 'tis time ta get up. We need ta be leaving fer work soon."

CHAPTER FIVE

No Crying Over Spilled Root Beer

A week or two after I started working at the factory, I was getting used to the way things were. All that means is that I wasn't crying as much. I absolutely hated the long hours and endless work. Even my dreams were filled with chickens and factory rooms and being yelled at by Mr. Reed or Mrs. Fredericks. They were horrible dreams that kept me awake at night or woke me before I needed to be up. I was still depressed and missing my friends so much it hurt. Anna was great, but even a new friend couldn't take away the ache of wishing things could go back to the way things used to be.

Still, I had a job to do. There was no way out. Every morning, my stomach would get all knotted up the minute I saw the factory gates. Most of that was because of Mr. Reed. He was mean to everyone, but he especially disliked me for some reason. I think it's because I did cry a lot, and he saw that as a sign of weakness and wanted to take advantage of that to make himself feel superior. Sometimes it honestly felt like he'd sit in his office and invent ways to get me in trouble.

Like this one time, I went to get the morning chickens from the cooler. I laid down my scrub brush on a table next to the doors so I could grab the cart with both hands and steer it better. I pushed it to the vats, and Anna immediately grabbed one of the chickens and began cleaning. I grabbed one, too, but that was when I realized I'd left the scrub brush behind.

"Oh, blast," I said to Anna. "I'll be right back. I left my brush."

She laughed. "Not awake yet, are ya?"

I ran back to the table, grabbed it, and took about two steps when Mr. Reed started yelling at me.

"Sundo!" he boomed. "Why are you just now getting to work? The whistle sounded ten minutes ago!"

"Oh, it's ok, Mr. Reed," I said, using my manners. "I was on time, but I just forgot my scrub brush and had to come back to get it."

"Don't you lie to me! I saw you. You have your scrubber in your hand!"

I stood there for a moment. Seriously? Didn't he realize that he just proved my point? Didn't he see that I was wearing my coat and boots?

So I tried again.

"That's what I mean, sir. I'm just heading back to the vats. I was here on time. Mum and Anna can tell you-"

"I don't need to talk to them. Get over to Mrs. Fredericks and tell her you are ten minutes late. And don't give me any more of your excuses!"

"But Mr. Reed, I'm not-"

"Now!" he bellowed.

Immediately I lowered my head and started for her office. I wasn't about to take any chances. I saw him hit a lady, and I didn't want to be next. Looking over my shoulder, I could see he was following me just to make sure I did it.

Mrs. Fredericks gave me a lecture about the sins of tardiness and how we all have to do our parts and that includes being on time, blah blah blah.

Then she and Mr. Reed said they were going to dock my pay by a nickel. Finally, I was allowed to leave.

"Where on earth have ya bean?" Anna asked. I noticed she had done about a half a cart of chickens by herself.

I told her the whole story, and ended with, "You know, he wasted more time making me go get a lecture than I would have wasted if I'd actually been late. That's stupid!"

"Aye-yah. Reed's an eejit, but at least ya didn't lose yer job."

She had no idea how much I wanted to lose the job, but I guessed she was right. I couldn't let Mum down. We had to have the money.

June was coming, and the days were getting warmer and longer. I'd grown accustomed to the long hours and was less tired at the end of the day. When work was over, I'd take off my shoes and socks and walk on the sidewalks that had been baking in the sun all day. It was a glorious feeling of release after being cooped up all day in the dark factory. Best of all, there was still sunshine and time to visit with friends or sit on the porch with my family after dinner. It was the only time I felt calm.

It was during one of those happy evenings when Mum and I were sitting on the porch, and she said, "Oh, wouldn't it be nice to have some lemonade?"

"Ooh, that would be nice. I can make some."

"All right, and we need to start makin' plans for some root beer as well."

"Root beer? Really?" We only got to drink root beer at Christmas or on the Fourth of July.

"I didn't think we'd be getting any this year, though," I thought aloud.

"Why not?" she asked.

"Well, the Fourth is on a Friday this year, and I don't think Mr. Reed will let us have any at the plant."

Mum laughed. "We don't have ta go ta work on the Fourth."

"We don't?" I shrieked. Joyous thoughts of having a day of freedom away from work filled my heart. And a three-day weekend away from Mr. Reed? It was almost more than my soul could handle.

I danced around the porch as a sudden thought entered my mind. "Does this mean we can go to the picnic as well?"

There had been a grand Independence Day picnic at Munson Park for as long as I could remember. There would be food, contests, foot races, and root beer. Plus, I'd be able to see some of my friends again; friends I hadn't seen since I left school in March.

"Can we, Mum?"

"I don't see why not. And ya can invite Anna along if ya wish."

"Truly?" I squealed out again. "That'll be perfect!"

I practically danced my way inside and into the kitchen to start on the lemonade, then Mum came after me, thinking aloud as she walked.

"I suppose we should be starting on the root beer this weekend, then. Just be mindful ya and yer father don't drink it in one day."

I laughed. Papa was notorious for sneaking off with some of the root beer bottles.

"I'll talk with yer Aunt Martha about helping. We can make a day of it."

We spent the evening plotting and planning what we wanted to do for Saturday. I hoped Aunt Martha would join us. Whenever she helped, she would bring the ingredients from the store that she and Uncle Randall owned, and we could make twice as much as usual. And sometimes she brought extra sweets.

By Wednesday, all the plans had been finalized, and by Friday everything was ready. I even woke up early on Saturday so I could hurry through my usual chores. I started some biscuits and tea for breakfast, then ran through the dusting and preparing the laundry. After we finished breakfast, I cleaned the dishes while Mum went out to hang up some clothes on the clothes line. There was a knock on the door and Aunt Martha appeared, carrying two sacks of ingredients.

"Hello, Beth!" she said. "How are ya doing now?"

"I'm fine," I told her as she hugged me. "Mum and Papa are doing better now, too."

She smiled. "I imagine they are as yer brother's begun writing home. What's he said lately?"

"Well, not much. All I know is he's in Oklahoma or perhaps Texas. He seems to be really secretive about what he's doing, but at least he's working. I don't know what the big secret is, though."

"Hmm," she mused. "I don't know of any secrets, but I can tell ya that I'm going to beat the boy when he gets home. Running away in the middle of the night, putting yer folks through this? When he gets home, I'm going to hug him, then wring his neck!"

I grinned as I finished drying off a plate. "You can do that after Papa and I finish with him first."

She just smiled and asked, "Where's yer mum?"

"I think she's in the backyard, putting clean clothes on the line. When I finish here, I'm going to the butcher shop. Is there anything I can get for you?"

"Aye-yah, as a matter of fact," she said, digging around in her bag, "I seem ta have forgotten the vanilla. So if I give ya some money, could ya pick it up for me?"

"Sure," I told her. "But you don't need to give me money. I have a job now. I think I can afford one bottle of vanilla."

"Oh, no ya don't. If I hadn't forgotten, ya'd not need ta be going to the store. Besides, ya'll be having ta put up with yer cousin Dennis tonight, and that'll be payment enough."

"All right," I laughed. I knew Denny could be a handful at times. "I'm done here, so could you let Mum know I'm leaving?"

"Sure," she said, "but before ya go, take this with ya and enjoy." She handed me a small bag. I looked inside. Sure enough, small chocolates. I knew she'd bring something.

"Thank you so much, Aunt Martha!" I said as I hurried out the door.

It was a beautiful day. The sun was warm, the wind was just right, and I felt so grown up going into town by myself. I savored my chocolates, made my way to the stores, and made my purchases. I was practically euphoric as I entered the butcher shop and saw Mr. Heckle busily cutting meat.

"Good morning, Mr. Heckle!"

"Hey, Missy, I haven't seen you here in a while," he said with a wide grin and friendly tone. "What can I do for you?"

I handed him Mum's note. "I need to pick up some roast beef for tonight's dinner."

"That's fine," he said as he looked over the order. "Where have you been hiding these days? Sylvia says she hasn't seen you or your brother in school lately."

I froze. Mr. Heckle was such a wonderful man, and I knew he was trying to be nice, but I didn't really want to tell him I had to quit school.

He stared at me over his glasses.

"Well, Dale's working for the Civilian Conservation Corps," I stammered.

"Oh, that's nice. And what about you, Missy?" I felt my face flush. "I've been busy."

Still he waited for a real answer. All my joy drained out of me at that moment.

"I'm working at the Hillerman Chicken Factory," I told him quietly.

He stared at me in disbelief. "What? Your parents are allowing you to work there?"

Tears started welling up in my eyes again, threatening to give away the fact that I'm not as strong as I wish I was. I wanted to pretend everything was fine in my life, like my world hadn't fallen apart, but it had.

I didn't want to talk about the job, or how pathetic it was. I didn't want to tell him how Dale and I had heard our parents fighting, and that was the night he ran away from home. He didn't need to know how much Mum cried or how worried Papa was.

After a very uncomfortable moment, he went back to his work. "How do you like it?" he said, looking over his glasses again.

"It's fine. It's a little, uhm…" I faltered. He looked like he was interested, so I finished with a quick, "It's all right."

He acted like he didn't believe me, not that I could blame him, but at least he quit talking and worked on my order. Deep inside, I felt like he was thinking poorly of my folks. I didn't ask him, though, because I wasn't sure I wanted to know.

I looked out the windows and thought about how it wasn't Papa's fault he couldn't find a job. He was always looking for one. He'd even found work digging ditches, but the employment contract only lasted a couple of weeks. Sometimes people said they wouldn't hire him because he "still had his Italian accent" and they "didn't hire foreigners." I couldn't even tell he had an accent at all, but that is what they would say. It wasn't fair, and it wasn't Papa's fault, yet I couldn't tell Mr. Heckle that. I just paid for the meat and left.

The walk home was much slower than it had been earlier that morning, so by the time I got home, Mum and Aunt Martha had already started combining the ingredients and preparing the dinner. I gave them the ingredients and sat down and listened as they chatted happily, bustling about the kitchen. After a while, I went down into the cellar to get the empty pop bottles. We had about two dozen of them that I'd been saving for a while. I decided that if I ever needed money quickly, I could sell them back to the store. I grabbed the wooden bottle crate and moved it out to the center of the floor, dusted the bottles, and took them upstairs to be cleaned with a bottle brush.

My spirits began to lift as soon as I came back into the kitchen. The smell of the root beer, the sound of laughter, the feel of the suds on my hands, they all made the sorrows of the morning slip away.

In the early afternoon, Uncle Randall showed up with Dennis. With three of us women working in the kitchen, there wasn't enough room for everyone, so they left with Papa. Personally, I think Mum just told them to go away so they wouldn't be under foot.

I, on the other hand, got to stay. I felt so grown up.

I was 14, I had a job, and I got to spend the afternoon scurrying about the kitchen laughing and talking and gossiping with my mum and aunt. They told the funniest stories about growing up.

Finally, everything had been measured and blended, and we took a taste. It wasn't quite ready yet, but it was almost done. We poured the drinks into the freshly cleaned bottles, then Mum added a hint of yeast to each one and placed them by the radiator.

"Mum, why are we putting them there?" I asked. "It's summer, and we won't be using the radiator."

"We can turn it on just a little. We have to keep it warm or it won't ferment in time. And don't ferget to take off the lids and maybe shake the bottles at least once a week, or we'll have a mess on our hands."

"Yes ma'am," I told her. I knew the root beer had to ferment, and the bottles needed to be shaken for the ingredients to stay mixed properly. I knew all about removing the lids to let out the gas produced by the fermentation process before mixing the ingredients, too. I decided the best thing to do was to come in after work each Friday, remove all the lids, and mix each bottle before returning them to their places. It would be easy.

We were almost through cleaning up the kitchen when Papa and Uncle Randall burst through the door with Denny.

"Margaret!" Papa called out so excitedly that I thought something was wrong.

"Margaret! I got a job! I got a job at the bank!"

He was so proud and excited that he could barely contain himself. The words flooded out so fast I almost couldn't understand him.

"I have a job cleaning the bank after everyone else has gone home for the day. It'll only be for a while, but Honey, it's a job!"

"Anthony, that's wonderful!" Mum cried, throwing her arms around him.

"It'll only be for a while, though. The man who usually does it is real sick, and I'll only be taking over for him while he is out, but I'll be working. And the best part is that I'll still have my days free to look for a permanent job."

"Let's celebrate!" Aunt Martha said. "Dinner is just about ready, and I brought a cake for dessert. Let's eat!"

Everyone was talking, laughing, clanking dishes and glasses. They were grabbing silverware and filling glasses with water. It was the first time in a long time that I had begun to feel hope again.

Wouldn't Mr. Heckle be proud of my family now? I wondered.

It's so strange how, when something good is going to happen, time seems to take forever. The next few weeks were long and difficult. Mr. Reed and Mrs. Fredericks were on a streak of terror, bullying everyone they could find. One day was particularly bad because Anna was out sick. Being the mean-spirited person she was, Mrs. Fredericks put Harold at my cleaning vat for the day. All he did was complain and insult Anna the entire time. He was awful.

July finally came, and it was the day before the picnic. I was in the kitchen, gathering food for the picnic basket when I noticed a problem.

I was positive we'd made twenty-four bottles of root beer because I remembered thinking that I had an even two dozen. I counted again but there were only twenty-three. I looked around the kitchen, wondering if one had leaked or if Mum had just wanted to taste one. But there were no bottles on the counter.

I stuck my head into the living room. "Mum, did we lose one of the pop bottles? Did one break or something?"

Mum looked perplexed. "No, why? Is one of them missing?"

"Yes." I didn't want to say it, but I had to. "You don't think Dennis took it, do you?"

"Took what?" Papa said as he entered the room to get ready to go to his job. He sat down and started to put on his shoes. "What did Denny take?"

"One of the bottles of root beer," I told him. "When we poured it a few weeks ago, I could've sworn they were all there but now there's only twenty-three."

"Oh, that wouldn't be Denny," he said, putting on his other shoe. "I took one."

"When did ya do that?" Mum asked as she went back to work on her sewing.

"Right after you made them," he replied casually. "I wanted to keep one for myself for after the picnic. Why?"

"Well, Papa, I was just going to shake it up."

He gave me a funny look. "Why?"

Mum chuckled. "Oh, Anthony, with the recipe that I use, ya need ta take off the lid every now and then to let out the fermented gasses. Then ya need ta shake the bottle ta make sure the ingredients are well mixed. Ya should know that. When was the last time ya let the cap off and shook it up?"

"I didn't know about that. I have it right here behind the couch," he said, reaching down to get the hidden bottle. "I'll shake it up for you," he said. "No big problem."

As he lifted the bottle and started to shake it, Mum jumped up and yelled, "Anthony, no!"

"What?" he answered, but it was too late. The bottle cap came flying off and a shower of the sticky drink gushed out, drenching him and Mum in the brown, sugary liquid, leaving a trail all over their hair and clothes. Everyone screamed, and then there was dead silence.

We stood there, quietly, staring at the mess. I snorted, trying to hold back the laughter. Papa chuckled, then Mum burst out laughing. In a rush of giggles, we all laughed and laughed.

"Well, it's a good thing I still have time before I have to be at work," Papa said.

"I'll go down inta the cellar and get the washtub and bring it up for ya," Mum said. "And Beth, ya need ta start gathering towels and start on this mess."

As she started down the basement stairs, we could hear her laughing, and Papa looked at the almost-empty bottle. "Well, here's to you my dear!" he said, and he drank down the little that was left.

I think that even when I become an adult, I'll think about root beer and my father, and I'll laugh.

CHAPTER SIX

The Picnic

My alarm clock never had the chance to go off the next morning. I was already awake, too excited to sleep. It was going to be the best Fourth of July ever. I'd run into my friend, Sarah, and she said several of the girls were meeting up at three to go get some ice cream. So that meant I could meet up with Anna in the morning, watch some of the races, eat, meet up with my friends for ice cream, and go back to the park later that night to watch fireworks. It would be so much fun.

But the thing that made it so wonderful was that I didn't have to work, and I had Three. Whole. Days. Away from Mr. Reed.

Jumping out of bed, I rushed through my breakfast and ran back upstairs to get dressed. I fished out my best dress from the closet, a blue plaid with a dropped waist and a white lace collar. It was the only truly nice dress I had, and I hadn't been able to wear it anywhere but church in the longest time.

When I grabbed my brush, I started to braid my hair, but then I had a thought. I'd been braiding it every single day since I'd started at the factory, and I wanted to do something different. I combed it out and pulled it back with two beautiful mother-of-pearl combs that my great-aunt had sent me from Ireland.

Because I'd been wearing it in a braid for so many days, I hadn't realized just how long it had grown. It was long enough that it pulled some of the curl out, making it look rather straight. I loved it! My hair has always been too curly, so this was perfect. And it made me look older. Well, I hoped so anyhow. If being short made me look younger, hopefully the hairstyle would make me look at least my age.

But the minute I got downstairs, I began to question myself. Papa didn't mean to, but he made me feel self-conscious.

"My, my. My little girl looks all grown up!"

"I do?" Suddenly, I wasn't sure I wanted to look grown. What if, instead of just looking nice, I looked like a little girl playing "dress up" in her mom's stuff? Would that make me look even younger?

"Uhm, I'll go back upstairs and braid my hair," I told Mum.

"Why on earth would ya do that? Ya look fine, and we need ta get going."

Hesitantly, I helped Mum finish the sandwiches, then we grabbed some of the root beer and left.

The fair was held at the city square each year, and it was already getting crowded. People were wandering around, looking to claim a spot for their picnic blankets. The area near the courthouse was most popular because it would provide more shade as the day grew warmer.

Once we found our spot, I strolled towards the gazebo to find Anna. I took the long way, near the contest tents and the race area, hoping to see some of my other friends, but I didn't see anyone I knew. It was still early, so I gave up and went to the gazebo. A band was playing "God Bless America," so

I just enjoyed the music while I waited. Suddenly, I realized Anna was standing next to me.

"There you are!" I squealed. "You must have been hiding."

"I saw ya from the other side of the gazebo," she said. "I was'nat sure 'twas ya because I've never seen ya with yer hair down. I like it. 'Tis pretty."

"You don't think it looks silly?"

"Silly? Are ya as mad as a box of frogs?"

"No, I'm not crazy," I laughed.

"Well, ya must be because I've got me own hair down, ya know."

She did. Her red hair just flowed into curls down her back, and she was even more beautiful than usual.

"Yeah, but you already look your age. I always look like a little kid."

"Nah," she said. "That's nothing ta do with yer hair. That's because y'er short!"

"Hey!"

She had a wicked gleam in her eye, and I couldn't help but laugh. It's true after all.

That's something I admired about Anna. She had the ability to pick on me, yet it came off funny and endearing. Not many people can do that. Usually, teasing is mean-spirited, but it was truly funny when Anna teased.

"So," she said, looking around, "this looks ta be a grand picnic, and a lot o' fun. What are we ta be doin' first?"

I thought it over. "Well, the games won't be starting for another hour. We could just stay here and listen to the music, or we could go over to all the baking and sewing contests if you want. Oh, and I definitely want to watch the foot races at ten, all right?"

"That sounds grand," she said. "Let's go see the sewing contests, yeah?"

We ended up talking through two more songs before we drifted toward the tents on the other side of the city square. They were tall, red and white striped tents with flaps opening on all the sides. Inside the first one was the quilting contest. There were beautiful quilts and coverings with bright, joyful colors and fancy stitching designs. I noticed Anna looking them over carefully.

"This is some fine handiwerk. Perhaps I could be makin' somethin' fer this contest next year," she mused.

I was astonished. "Do you know how to make a quilt?"

She giggled. "O' course. Don't ya?"

"No," I confessed. "I don't really have the patience for sewing."

"Don't be feelin' bad. Ya know how ta cook and I'm terrible at it."

"Really?" I was a bit surprised.

"Aye-yah, and I need ta be learnin' quickly or twill be a shock ta me beau."

"Why?"

Anna blushed and grabbed me by the arm, leading me out of the tent. "I think he's goin' ta ask me ta marry him," she whispered excitedly.

"Oh, my goodness!" I cried. "Do you really think so? When? Are you sure? But you're only 17! What will your papa say?" In the excitement, I was barraging her with questions.

"Well, I'm not sure, mind ya," she said slowly, "but Mum says he did ask ta speak with me papa. Besides, I will be 18 soon, ya know, and 'twouldn't be too soon. I do plan on waitin' till I'm nineteen. I'm not crazy, ya know. And I still need ta learn how ta cook."

I squealed and hugged her. We resumed our walk so we could talk and gossip freely, giving her the chance to tell me all about her beau. His name was Fred, and even though he wasn't an immigrant like her, his family had still been hit hard by this "Great Depression" as everyone else.

"So of course, we won't be havin' a big church affair," she told me, "but the priest of me church had done me cousin's weddin' at her house, so I think he kin do one at mine."

Then she sort of cocked her head and looked at me. "And if we do that, would ya like ta be me attendant?"

I was shocked. "Of course!" The thought of being a bridesmaid was the most thrilling thing I could think of. "I'd love to!"

And just like that, Anna had become my first friend to be thinking about marriage. As little girls, my friends and I talked about getting married someday to some boys we had crushes on, but this was my first serious, adult conversation with someone who really would be getting married. It was exciting and new, and there was so much about weddings that I'd never thought about. There wasn't a lot of money to go around, so it wouldn't be like the pictures of the rich socialites I'd seen in the newspapers, but it was still fun to think about.

"And me mum has her weddin' dress in her hope chest," she was saying. "I think we kin sew some new lace on the torn parts. Maybe ya would like ta come help us out?"

I laughed. "I don't sew, remember? I cook."

"Well then, ya kin come over ta my house and cook while Mum and I are sewing; how's that?"

"Deal."

"I think 'tis wonderful that ya already know how ta cook so ya kin cook fer yer husband whenever ya get married someday."

"If I get married," I corrected.

"Ya told me once about a boy ya like. Don't ya ever think of cooking fer him?"

"For Tomic? No, he's Dale's friend, and I don't think he even knows I'm alive."

"What?" she looked confused. "What's 'is name?"

I giggled. "It's pronounced 'Toe-meek.' It's an Italian name, but the American version is Tommy. You could call him that if it's easier."

She shrugged. "So, what makes ya think Tommy does'nat know ye're alive? If he's yer brother's best friend, surely he knows ya."

"I guess that's true, but I think he just thinks of me as his friend's pesky little sister. Or just one of his dad's patients. His dad is our doctor, Dr. Viosca."

About that time, we arrived at the picnic tables under the trees and were able to see the start of the pie-eating contest. Several young men were around a table with their hands tied behind their backs, waiting. When the pop-gun went off, they began eating away at the pies in front of them. The crowd cheered and howled with laughter as blueberries and juice covered their faces. People were screaming and cheering for different contestants, but we didn't know any of the boys, so we just watched and laughed.

The whole thing sort of made me sad, though, because I knew my brother, Dale, would've entered that race, and I would have been cheering him on. There was part of me that was missing him so much right then, and there was a part of me that was angry for the way he was making me and my parents feel, and for what he was putting us through.

I pushed aside all those thoughts and asked Anna if she wanted to go with me to the tents to see Mum. She'd decided to enter the Jams and Jellies Competition at the last minute and I wanted to know how she did. She didn't think she had a chance, but I think she's a great cook.

We found her standing by Aunt Martha, waiting for the announcement of the judges. "How do ya think it went?" Anna asked.

Mum shrugged. "I don't know. They tasted me jam twice, but they tasted Mrs. O'Hara's three different times."

"But that could be anything," Aunt Martha reassured. "Maybe they were trying to see if she should win third place. Who knows?"

We waited and waited. Finally, an older man in worn-out overalls and a white shirt came to the middle of the tent. "Ladies and gentlemen," he began, "we are ready to announce the winners. The third place winner is Mrs. Herbert Benefield!"

We clapped politely as a sweet little old lady came up to claim her prize. Then he continued. "The second place, red ribbon goes to Mrs. Anthony Sundo!"

We screamed and cheered as Mum walked over to accept her prize It was a lovely red ribbon with a big number 2 on it, and a shiny new fifty cent piece for a prize.

"And the winner of the Blue Ribbon and the two dollars in prize money goes to… Mrs. Robert O'Hara!"

Everyone cheered for her as she took her prizes. Of course, I thought my mum should have won, but I was pretty proud that she came in second place with a last-minute entry. I was glad to be learning from her.

The pie contest was next, but I wasn't really interested in that, so Anna and I decided to go ahead and walk over to the foot races. Those are always exciting, especially when the older, more handsome boys were running. But the little boys always ran first, so we took our time getting there.

"Oh, my!" Anna said suddenly.

"What?" I asked, startled.

"I'm thinking ya might have an admirer," she answered, still staring at something in the distance.

"What?" I followed her gaze, then I spotted someone standing by the lemonade stand. He wore a white shirt and a pair of brown suspenders. His dark hair was shimmering in the sunlight, and he seemed more like a man than the boy I'd last seen at school. When our eyes met, he smiled, waved, and began walking toward us. I looked around to see who he was waving at, but when I didn't see anyone, I waved back.

"I can't believe this!" I said in a rush of whispers. "It's him! It's the boy I was telling you about—you know, my brother's best friend, Tommy? That's him!"

"You're tasin' me! That's him?"

"Yes! And he's coming over here!"

She looked him over, and a smile crossed her face. "My, but he is handsome. I kin understand yer interest in him."

"Hello, Beth!" he said as he approached. "I thought that was you, but I wasn't sure at first. How are you doing?"

"I'm fine," I replied shyly. "How are you?"

"Doing well, doing well. I've been busy, but nothing too interesting. What about you? I haven't seen you around much. You been busy, too?"

I was so embarrassed. Why did he have to ask that?

Fortunately, Anna came to my rescue when she nudged me in the ribs.

"Oh, yes! Tommy, this is one of my best friends, Anna. Anna, this is Tommy."

"Glad to meet you, Anna," he said, shaking hands with her.

"And ya too," she replied.

"That's a lovely accent. Where are you from?"

"I was born and raised in Ireland," she beamed. "We've only bean living here in Pittsburgh for the last couple o' years."

"That's one of the places I want to visit someday. It sounds like such an interesting country. I've heard about kissing the Blarney Stone, and I thought that would be something fun to do, just to say I did it."

"Oh, 'tis such a lovely country. I've never been to Blarney Castle meself, but there are so many other stories I could be tellin' ya about the country and the people."

"We might need to do that sometime," he said, but then he turned his attention back to me. "So, where did you disappear to? I haven't seen you at school in ages."

I was mortified. Why'd he ask that? I didn't want to tell him that I had a job cleaning the dirt and feathers off chickens. Yet he stood there, waiting for an answer.

"I had to go to work," I said simply.

"Really?" He looked genuinely concerned. "Where are you working? What do you do?"

My face reddened. I know it did, because I could feel it. "I work at the Hillerman Chicken Factory."

"Doing what?" he asked, obviously astonished.

I started to say something, but nothing came out. Anna must have known how embarrassed I was because she broke in with the most wonderful statement I'd ever heard.

"Beth and I work at the final cleanin' vats," she declared in a most dignified manner. "We're the ones who make sure an' certain the chickens are ready fer processin.' If we weren'nat there, the canned birds might be makin' someone sick, and since they're being sent ta our army boys overseas," and she paused for emphasis, "well, I'm just glad Beth is there ta be helpin' me."

Looking at her, I almost burst out laughing. She'd made my job seem so noble and important. But there was no way I was going to let Tommy know just how pathetic it really was. Geez, we only cleaned chickens for a living!

Tommy, however, looked thoroughly impressed. "That sounds like such a difficult job for ladies so young as you two, but I suppose you must be quite good at it."

Then he continued. "Well, I'll be running in one of the races in a few minutes. Are you going to be there? I could use someone to cheer for me."

"Of course!" I told him, happy to be off the subject of work.

"Good," he said with a smile. "I'll need all the help I can get. I might even be able to win since Dale isn't here this year."

Then his face fell a bit, and his cheeks turned slightly red. "Maybe I shouldn't have brought that up."

"Oh, it's fine," I said, waving it off.

"What do you hear from him?"

"He's working in Oklahoma or Texas, I think. I'm not sure. His letters have been very short lately, but he sends us some money almost every week."

"So I guess he's doing all right."

"I guess so. Seems to be."

I didn't want him to know I was still mad at Dale for leaving in the middle of the night like he did, but in a way,

I was beginning to understand why he did it. In his mind, I guess he was trying to help the family.

"Well, I do wish he was here," Tommy remarked. "When you write to him, let him know school's no fun without him."

"I will," I said, pretty much forcing a smile. After all, I wanted to be back in school, too. My heart ached, knowing they were out on summer vacation, and they got to see each other all the time, and even when school was back in session again, their school day would from eight to three-thirty. And mine was six in the morning to six in the evening. My heart so wished for things to be the way they used to be.

"Hey, Tommy!" someone called in our direction. I was glad, because I knew talking about school was going to make me cry again. "The foot races are about to start! Are you coming?"

He turned and called back, "I'll be right there!" Then he looked back at me. "Well, the race is about to begin, and if you cheer for me, I think I can win this one."

"All right, I promise." I smiled. When he smiled back at me, I knew I was blushing again, but I just couldn't help it.

"I'll see you after the race," he said as he headed toward the field. Then he turned and said, "By the way, I like your hair that way. It's really pretty!"

I was in shock, but Anna started laughing. "Oh, no, he doesn'nat even know ye're alive. Not at all!"

"I'm sure he just thinks of me as his friend's bratty little sister."

"I'm thinkin' ya need ta know more about men. He likes ya; that's what I'm thinkin'."

My heart was racing, too afraid to let me get my hopes up. "No, I don't think so."

She just gave me one of her looks that made me think she was up to something. "Aye-yah, I'm thinkin' he does. And we'd best be headin' over ta where we can see the race so ya can be cheerin' fer him."

We walked over to stand near the end of the finish line where we could see more easily. Well, I should say Anna walked. I floated over there. Tommy had said I was pretty! He had to win that race. He just had to!

"Good luck, Tommy!" I cried out as the boys lined up at the starting line, but I don't think he could hear me. Someone fired a starting gun, and the boys were off running. I yelled and yelled for Tommy as he closed in the leaders as they approached the finish line. There was a sudden roar from the crowd, and I realized another boy had sprinted ahead, passing Tommy and leaving the rest of the pack behind.

"No!" I screamed. "Run, Tommy!"

"Go, Tommy!" Anna yelled beside me.

I couldn't believe this was happening. He'd finally noticed me, and he just had to win. He just had to.

But then, just as suddenly as the boy had burst forth on the track, Tommy darted ahead and dove over the finish line and won!

Anna and I grabbed each other by the shoulders, jumping up and down.

"Let's go congratulate him," she suggested.

"I'd love to!" I told her, and we rushed over to the small crowd that gathered to congratulate the two boys. We pushed our way through the crowds, but when I saw him, I came to an abrupt stop.

My face must have drained all color because Anna looked at me and gave a startled, "What's wrong?" Then she turned and saw what I had seen. "Who's that?" she asked, clearly disgusted with the scene in front of her.

"That's Sadie. Sadie Moore. She's the same age as Tommy and Dale."

What I didn't have to tell her—it was quite obvious—was that she was also taller, prettier, and much richer than me. And at that moment, she was blatantly hugging Tommy. Then she kissed him on the cheek, right there in front of everybody.

When she finished with that, she tugged on his arm, urging him to follow her. He waved goodbye to me and left.

With her. That awful girl who thought she was better than everyone else. The one who yelled at me for trying to return a book.

Anna made a face. "Don't be worryin' about her, Beth. He wouldn'nat have a girl like that. She's a bit of a show-off, that one is. An' he said yer hair was lovely, an' 'tis."

There was nothing that could make me feel better at that moment. After all, Tommy was really Dale's best friend, and he probably really did think of me as a pesky little sister. Sadie was the same age as the boys and had everything I didn't. Why wouldn't he be with her?

"Come on," I said, admitting defeat in my head. "Let's go get some lunch."

"Aye-yah. Ya will feel better when ya eat."

"I'm not sure I could eat right now," I sighed. "But maybe I can drown my sorrows in some of Mum's root beer. Come on."

"Sounds good," she said as we walked to the grassy area where my parents had set up their picnic blanket.

My folks were there, sitting and talking. I introduced Anna to my papa, and we grabbed some food and a couple of bottles of the root beer. I was still pretty upset, so we went to eat underneath a nearby oak tree where we could talk in private. All through lunch I picked at my food, but Anna chatted on happily. She kept making jokes about rich people that would make me laugh. She said things like how Sadie could afford to buy a scrub brush but wouldn't know how to use it. Then she said Sadie only liked fishing because she thought goldfish were made out of real gold, and how there should be money in the river "banks." Before long, we were talking about other things, too, and she was making me laugh even more.

Suddenly, she exclaimed, "Oh! Tis almost two o'clock! Would ya like ta come meet me beau? He's going ta meet me here ta walk me home."

"Really? He's here?"

"Aye-yah. He had to work this morning, so we made plans ta walk home tagether. Want ta meet him?"

"Sure!" I said. We cleaned up our mess and headed back to the gazebo area.

The day was warm, and the band wouldn't be playing until three, so there weren't many people there. Anna spotted him almost immediately.

"Fred! Hallo!" she called out.

A nice-looking man turned around and smiled at us. He was taller than Anna, but not too tall, and he had light brown hair. He wasn't overly handsome, but when he looked at Anna, his face lit up, and I could see exactly what Anna found so attractive about him.

"Anna, there you are! I've been waiting for you."

"But 'tis just now two o'clock," she said, looking at her watch.

"I know," he answered, "but I got off work early and just couldn't wait to see you."

She giggled, and he grabbed her around the waist and hugged her. Silently, I stood by, wishing I had a boyfriend.

"Fred, I want ya ta meet me best friend, Beth. She's the one I've been telling ya about who works with me at the plant."

Fred turned and extended his hand. "Hello, Beth. I've heard so much about you. It's nice to meet you."

I shook hands with him. "Nice to meet you, too, Fred."

Then it suddenly hit me that this man must have been at least 20. I spent so much time with Anna that I often forgot she was older than me, and it would make sense that her boyfriend would be a bit older than her. But I never realized how much older he would be than me.

I suddenly felt like a little kid, hanging around with two grown-ups.

It wasn't anything Anna or Fred did, but the realization that I was still just a 14-year-old kid in a grown-up world.

And being less than five feet tall and overly skinny made me look, and therefore feel, even more like a kid.

"Would you like to accompany Anna and me to see the next band play?" he asked.

"I'd love to," I lied, "but I'm supposed to meet some friends from my old school. I really should be going."

"Are ya sure?" Anna asked.

Even though I had plenty of time, I said, "Yeah, I'd better go find them before everyone starts leaving. I'll see you at work Monday."

"All right," she said. "I'll see ya then."

I left the gazebo and decided to go see if I could find some of my friends. That way, it wouldn't be lying, and I could catch up on the school gossip. It seemed like a good plan at the time.

CHAPTER SEVEN
No Fireworks for Me

I was wrong.

A few girls were already sitting at a picnic table under a tree, and I could see that one of them was Sarah, so I waved at her. The other two girls turned to see who she was waving at, and I smiled as soon as I realized one was Allison, a really sweet girl in my English class.

Then my stomach lurched. Sitting beside her was the one person I didn't want to see, Sadie.

I couldn't very well walk off when I realized it was her. It would have been obvious and rude. Worse than that, it would have given her another reason to be nasty to me. So, I just smiled and walked on ahead.

Everyone started chatting at the same time.

"Beth!" Allison cried. "We haven't seen you in ages!"

"I'm so glad you could come!" Sarah said. "I'm glad you didn't have to work today."

"Where've you been?" Allison asked.

"Oh, just working," I told her, quickly brushing the question aside. I started asking them about school, and other friends, and everything seemed great for a few minutes. Then, the question came up again.

"So, tell us," Sadie said with a devious gleam in her eye, "you say you're working? Where?"

"Oh, nowhere," I mumbled.

"Where?" she asked again.

I glared at her. "At the Hillerman Chicken Factory." There was a brief, uncomfortable silence.

"Are there any cute boys there?" Allison asked. I'm sure she asked because she knew that a silly statement might help to break the tension between Sadie and myself.

I laughed and told her no. "There's really only one guy our age, and he's horrible. Other than that, it's a bunch of old women and me. But there is this girl named Anna, who's the same age as-"

"What do you do there?" Sadie continued.

"Anna's actually a little bit older than us," I continued in a feeble attempt to ignore her.

"I said, 'What do you do there,' Beth?" she repeated forcefully, her smile still icy.

I remembered what Anna had said to Tommy, and I stood up straight. "Anna and I are at the final cleaning vats. We have the last say in how clean the meat is before it is canned, which is very important because our canned chickens are sent to the military men overseas. Now, if you'll excuse me, I just came to chat for a little bit because I have to meet Anna in a while. I'll see you later."

"I wish you could stay," Sarah said, but I told her I couldn't and left.

Maybe it's wrong to lie, but I did it anyway. I knew I couldn't stand to be around Sadie one moment longer. She'd have me in tears before we ever even made it to the ice cream shop, and I wasn't going to let that happen. And besides, that was when I realized I had nothing in common with these girls anymore anyway, so why should I stay?

With my head high and my shoulders back, I walked away as nonchalantly as I could, but then I heard Sadie laughing.

"How grand is that?" she asked the girls. "Does she really think she's so important? I clean chickens for my mother all the time. Maybe I should send mine 'to the military men overseas!'" she mimicked. Then she laughed like it was the funniest thing she'd ever heard.

I don't get people like Sadie. Here she was; pretty, smart, and wealthy, yet she had no compassion or sympathy for others. I guess that whole stock market crash a few years ago didn't affect her, so she didn't care. Across the country, people were out of jobs, families were split, and people were starving, but her world never changed.

Maybe I had a job I hated, and there were people there I didn't like, but I was doing it to keep my family together. My brother had already run away from home, and Papa had said he was thinking of leaving to find work, too, so I had to do whatever I could to keep the rest of us together.

I understood why Mum made me take that job. I'd never admit it to her of course, but I understood.

But Sadie? I don't know if she'll ever understand. I realized that in some ways, I even felt a bit sorry for her. Until some tragedy hits her family, she'll never understand what real life is like, and that's a hard way to learn about what a family does for each other.

I walked back to the picnic area and helped Mum clean up. Grabbing one bottle of root beer, I told her I was heading home ahead of her and Papa. I wanted the time alone. I wanted to cry, and I didn't want anyone there when I did.

CHAPTER EIGHT
Pranks and Problems

A couple of weeks later, Anna and I were at our vats when Mum came over and asked Anna to take some papers to Mrs. Fredericks' office. She wiped her hands on a towel, delivered the papers, and returned a few minutes later. We never thought anything of it until about an hour later.

Mrs. Fredericks came storming into our area and began yelling at Mum. I could hear her from where I was standing at the vats. I was scared for her, so I walked around the other side of the transport cart to get a better look.

"Where are they?" she demanded as she stomped her feet. She looked more like a little kid demanding sweets than a grown adult who was supposed to be a supervisor.

"Mrs. Sundo, where are those lists I wanted? I wanted them by 10:30, and it is almost noon! I ought to dock your pay!"

Mum looked really surprised. "I sent them to ya over an hour ago."

"Well, I don't have them," she said smugly, crossing her arms in front of her chest like she'd just won an argument.

Mum took a deep breath, and I could see she was struggling with her temper. Then she called over to us. "Anna, come here please."

Most of the workstations around us had become quiet, wondering what the problem was. I followed Anna over to where they were talking.

"Anna, where are those work reports I asked ya ta take ta Mrs. Fredericks?"

"I put them on her desk, just like ya asked," she said simply, but she was met with a blaze of anger from Mrs. Fredericks.

"You most certainly did not put them on my desk! I was just in there and they are nowhere to be seen! I said I wanted those reports on my desk by 10:30, and I'm taking twenty-five cents from each of your paychecks. And you!" she yelled at me. "What are you doing here? Get back to the vats or I'll dock your pay as well!"

I scurried back over to the vats as quick as I could, but not before I heard Mum saying, "I'm sure Anna could show ya where they are," in a cool, calm voice.

"Aye-yah, I can do that," Anna offered. She and Mum walked toward the office with Mrs. Fredericks following and yelling at them all the way.

A few minutes later, Anna returned, laughing.

"What happened?" I whispered.

"I don'nat know. She might be goin' blind. They were right there on her desk in plain view! I don'nat see how she could be missin' them."

"Is she still going to dock your pay?"

"Nay, she can'nat do that, bein' as they were right there." But then she leaned down onto the vat and said, "Ya know, maybe this is a good thing, yeah?"

I was puzzled. "Why?"

"Because," she said with a giggle, "this may be meanin' that she's goin' off her noggin, an' they can be firin' her!"

We laughed, but then it happened again.

The next time Mum needed papers delivered to Mrs. Fredericks, she gave them to me instead. I decided to get it over with as quickly as I could because I didn't want her yelling at me like she had at Anna.

When I got to her office, she was humming and filing away some papers in a tall filing cabinet on the far side of the room. I marched in, put the papers on her desk, and left.

I went straight back to work, so I was surprised and dismayed to have Mrs. Fredericks come storming back as she had before, only this time she was yelling at me.

"I put them on her desk," I told Mum when she asked.

"That's impossible!" she bellowed, fury spilling out of her. "I've been in my office for the last two hours and I would've seen you."

"You were filing some papers, so maybe," I started out, but Mum interrupted with her calm, low voice.

"Could ya please show us where ya put the papers?"

"Of course," I agreed, trying to sound as calm as Mum, but there were tears already forming in my eyes. I walked to the office with Mum, Mrs. Fredericks, and Anna following me. I went straight to her desk, picked up the papers, and handed them to her.

Mrs. Fredericks stared blankly at them as Anna tried desperately to keep from giggling. Mum just looked at the papers.

"Is there anything else we can do fer ya, Mrs. Fredericks?" she asked.

Mrs. Fredericks, with a puzzled look on her face, gave a quiet, "No, no. That will be all. Thank you."

As soon as we were out of earshot, Mum mumbled, "I think the old lady's losing it!"

Anna whispered to me, "I wonder if she'd be needin' any help with that?"

I looked at her. "What?"

With a gleam in her eye, Anna giggled and began rushing back to the vats. I quickly followed, my tears quickly drying up. I knew she wanted to talk in private.

"I was just sayin', if Mrs. Fredericks is losin' her mind, what's wrong with us helpin' ta speed up the process?"

I didn't get what she was saying at first, but the more she talked, the more she schemed, and the more I vowed to help her.

The next day, Anna and I cleaned as many chickens as we could just as fast as we could while we waited for Mrs. Fredericks to pass by us. As soon as she did, we rushed to put the chickens in the refrigerated section and ran to her office. Anna went inside while I stood lookout by the door. After a few moments, she emerged, stuffing some papers into her firemen's boots. We giggled and headed back to the vats.

We wanted so badly to see some sort of reaction, but we had to be very patient. Finally, it paid off. She came rushing out of her office, looking everywhere for something. She wouldn't tell anyone what she was looking for, and she wouldn't accept any help from anyone. But we knew.

We tried our best not to giggle as she went by. As soon as she'd passed us, we ran back to her office where Anna returned the papers right where she'd found them. Then we got back to the vats before anyone could notice. It's a good thing we did, too, because just as we grabbed two chickens and put them in the water, Mr. Reed came walking by with Mrs. Fredericks close at his heels.

"How could you have been so stupid!" he yelled angrily.

"I can promise you that they did *not* fall into the wrong hands!" she retorted angrily. They paid no attention to us and continued yelling at each other as they disappeared down the hallway.

"And what do ya make of that?" Anna laughed. "How important could they be?"

We waited a couple more minutes, then snuck down to the end of the hallways and peeked around the corner. Mr. Reed had a relieved look on his face, and Mrs. Fredericks was incredulously staring down at the papers she'd just spent twenty minutes searching for. We laughed ourselves silly as we ran back to our workstation.

"Did ya see the look on her face?" Anna gasped between giggles.

"The best part was having Reed yelling at her," I replied. "Maybe he'll dock her pay for once! And what was that about them 'being in the wrong hands?' What are they, national secrets or something?"

"I don'nat know, but I know they weren'nat in 'the wrong hands.' They were'nat in anyone's hands. They were just in me boots!" She caught her breath and said, "I wonder what'll be disapperin' from her desk next?"

We decided to wait a few days before trying anything silly again. When we did, I stood lookout as before, and Anna snuck in to work her magic. As soon as she came out, we scurried back to the work area and began cleaning furiously.

"What did you do?" I asked once we were safely caught up on washing.

Her eyes sparkled. "I moved everything on her desk. If 'twas on the right, tis now on the left, and if 'twas on the left, tis now on the right. Tis mirror opposite of whatever it was."

I thought that was genius, but after a while, we realized we hadn't had a response from Mrs. Fredericks. If her desk had bothered her, she never let on about it. Subsequently, we concluded that our pranks needed to be a little more creative.

The next time we decided to see if we could get her, it was a lot harder. For two days, Anna and I would find excuses to "need" to walk past the office, often pretending to deliver papers or go get scrub brushes. Every time, she was working away at her desk.

Then finally, we saw her leave and we ran to put the unwashed chickens in the cooler and get to work on her office.

This time, I had Anna be the lookout while I went in, but I didn't really see much I could mess with. I was tired of looking at papers on her desk, but there wasn't much else of interest.

Then I saw the painting over her desk. It was a picture of a fancy house with some ladies drinking tea on a porch off to the side. I pulled up her chair, and standing on it, I reached up grabbed the frame, and flipped it upside down. All of the ladies were pointing down as smoke drifted out of the upside-down chimney. It was perfect.

I ran out of the office, grabbed Anna, and hurried back to the vats.

"Well?" she asked once we were safely working again.

"You know that picture that hangs over her desk?" She nodded. "I hung it upside down. You ought to see it!"

"That's marvelous! Ya clever thing! How long do ya think it'll take her ta figure out what's wrong? Do ya want ta wager on how long that'll be?"

"No, you know I don't gamble," I quipped. "But I hope it's after work when she does notice. I don't want to be around when she finds it."

For the next several days, we would conveniently "walk by" her office to sneak a look at the painting. We really figured she would find it within a day or two, but it was almost two weeks before she turned it back over!

There were several other pranks we played on her. Sometimes we would hide things, sometimes we would just move them. Once, over several days, we slowly pushed her office furniture closer and closer together, a little bit every day, to make the room appear to grow smaller and smaller. We didn't really expect her to notice the change, but she must have. One day she told Mum she was beginning to get out of her office more because it was "getting too stuffy."

"Maybe she needs ta be losing some weight," Mum grumbled after she was gone. We giggled, but Mum just looked at us. Then we decided to put the furniture back so she'd stay in her office—and away from us!

Sadly, the best trick Anna pulled was also, unfortunately, the one that got us in trouble with Mum.

Of Chickens and Hobos

Early one morning, Anna snuck into Mrs. Fredricks's office again. She was in there for quite a while, and I just knew we were going to get caught. When she finally came out, she motioned for me to follow her. We walked hastily, without a word.

"I know what I'm wantin' ta do," she began, "but I'm not quite sure just how ta get it done."

I knew by the gleam in her eye that this would be the best prank yet. "What? What is it?"

"Well, I'm wantin' ta fill her cup with cold water and put it high upon her shelves, so when she starts pullin' it down, she'll be dowsed with cold water!"

"Oh, that's hilarious! What's the problem?"

"When do we get the cup out and back in?"

"Well," I began formulating aloud, "I suppose what we really should do is just take in a cup of cold water after work and set the trap for the next day. It won't be cold, icy water, but it will still be cold enough to do the trick."

"That should do it," she said thoughtfully. "We'll just have to be more careful, because everyone will be gettin' off work, so there will be more people roamin' around. Then we're more likely to get caught."

"Not if we get to it just as the last whistle blows. Everyone will be going to the lockers to get out of their work clothes. And she doesn't lock her office until after she's out of her apron and heading for home, so that will give us an extra five minutes."

"That's brilliant," she told me. I was rather proud of that.

It was so hard to wait for the day to end, and it seemed to take forever. We talked about anything we could to get our minds off the clock. We discussed people at work, about my going back to school, and her and her boyfriend. We even chatted about how he'd already spoken to her father, hopefully about proposing.

We had to be perfect with our timing, so we conveniently finished up a tray of chickens with only a few minutes left before the whistle blew. That gave us a chance to put them in the coolers and grab a glass of water before sneaking over to Mrs. Fredericks's office. As soon as the whistle blew, she walked out, leaving the door wide open.

"Do you see it?" I whispered from my usual post at the door.

"Aye-yah. Tis right here," she said. She poured out the little bit of tea that was left into a potted plant, filled the cup with the water, and put it high on the shelf. The thought even crossed my mind how it was good to have Anna do the work since I'm too short to reach the shelf.

"Let's go!" she said as soon as she was finished.

We had to hurry to the lockers so Mum wouldn't notice that we were still wearing our boots and jackets. But I decided that, if she asked, I could just tell her we were at the coolers. It was the truth; just not the whole truth.

We hurried out of the building with everyone else.

"See you tomorrow," I told Anna.

She grinned. "And don't be forgettin' ta be here a little early if ya can," she whispered.

The next morning, Mum seemed to be in no hurry to get to work, but we eventually managed to get to the plant. Both Anna and I were in our boots and jackets when we saw Mrs. Fredericks heading past us towards our office. We waited, but nothing happened.

It wasn't until much later that she came back towards our area, and we could tell she was looking for something. She stopped by our station, where Mum was collecting cleaned chickens and asked, "Have you seen my teacup, Mrs. Sundo?"

"No," Mum answered a little curtly. I knew Mum hated that teacup. She'd often told me that she didn't think it was right that Mrs. Fredericks had tea any time she wanted, but no one else was allowed to have even a cup of water on the workroom floor. They were only allowed use the water cooler at the far end of the work room.

Then she headed to Mum's workstation, but the ladies there hadn't seen it either, so she went to search somewhere else. The entire time, she was complaining about getting old and forgetting things.

Anna and I worked away, quietly. I never saw her going back towards her office, but a few minutes later, a scream and a string of cusswords came pouring out the office door.

"I'll kill them!" she screamed as she bolted from her office, drops of water still dripping from her face and hair. "I will absolutely kill them! When I find out who is responsible for this, when I find out who's been in my office, they are dead! Do you hear me? They are dead!" With that, she turned and stomped away.

After a short, shocked silence, everyone else in the area looked at each other, wondering what had happened. Some laughed, some shook their heads, and some just shrugged their shoulders and went back to work. Unable to maintain our composure, Anna and I walked quickly to the ladies' restroom where we could both laugh aloud.

"Did ya see the look on her face?" Anna choked through the laughter. "She was castin' a kitten!"

"She sure was!"

We laughed and chuckled for several minutes, trying to calm ourselves down enough to return to work without anyone figuring out that we knew more than they did.

When we were finally able to leave the restroom, we headed straight back to the vats. But when we turned the corner, there was Mum. She was poised as if she'd been waiting on us.

We froze.

"So, ladies," she began slowly, "would ya like ta tell me how many of these strange occurrences have been yer idea? Or would ya prefer I make me own assumptions?"

I couldn't move. I just couldn't bear to tell Mum it was our fault. As usual, nothing stopped Anna from speaking her mind.

"'Tis mostly me ta blame, Mrs. Sundo. 'Twas me that came up with all the ideas ta drive Mrs. Fredericks off her noggin'. Elizabeth was havin' little ta do with it, ma'am."

"But Elizabeth did have something in the doing of these things, I take it?" She was staring quite hard by then.

"Yes, ma'am. I-, I was the look-out." That was all I could manage.

"So yer responsible for the tea cup? Fer moving furniture in the office?"

I looked at Anna, and I shouldn't have. She started snickering, and we both started laughing. "Yes ma'am."

"And fer turning the picture upside down?"

"Yes, ma'am."

"And for the missing weekly pay reports?"

We were suddenly very sober. "Missing pay reports?" Anna asked.

"Aye-yah. There are some work and pay reports that disappeared three days ago. Ya wouldn't know anything about that, would ya?"

"No, Mum."

"Nay, Mrs. Sundo. We did'nat do anything brutal. Only a bit of prankin'. We'd take nothing ta do with someone's work or pay checks; I can promise ya that."

Mum eyed us suspiciously. "All right then," she said, "but ya'd better be telling me the truth."

"We are, Mum. We wouldn't take anything that would affect someone's paychecks."

"O' course not, Mrs. Sundo. T'woudn't be right."

"Fine," Mum said with a sigh. "Now get back ta work, the both of ya. And no more fooling around. I can't afford fer ya to lose yer jobs. Especially ya, Elizabeth."

"Yes ma'am," I told her, and we walked solemnly back to the vats.

"I promise, an' I had no idea some work papers were gone missin'," Anna said. "It never dawned upon me that we'd be blamed for anythin' else that might be missin' or out o' order."

"Me, neither. Mum's right. We can't afford to lose our jobs."

We were a lot more somber after that, but for the next three days, we giggled every time we saw Mrs. Fredericks. We had to try to stay calm and pretend not to know what had happened.

To this day, I don't know how Mum knew we'd been the culprits trying to drive Mrs. Fredericks crazy. And we never found out where those missing pay reports went, either. Even now, sometimes I wonder, if we had not played these tricks, and if the papers had not gone missing, would things have gone the way they did?

CHAPTER NINE

A Visit with the Gypsies

By late August, Anna's wish—and my worst nightmare—had come true. On her 18th birthday, Fred had proposed marriage. I was happy for Anna, of course, because she was my first close friend to get engaged, and I was thrilled that she'd asked me to serve as her attendant, but I was kind of sad, too. Part of it was because I wanted to be old enough to have a boyfriend. Worse than that, though, was that she wouldn't be working at the factory anymore. Married women seldom worked outside the home unless their husbands were dying or out of work themselves. I felt that once she was gone, I'd be alone. Work wasn't much fun to begin with, but without Anna, it would be no fun at all. At least they were waiting a full year, so I had some extra time with her.

"Do you know what you're going to do about your wedding dress yet?" I asked one day as we were sitting outside eating lunch. It wasn't like there were many people who could afford a fancy dress. "Did your mum's dress fit you?"

Anna's eyes sparkled. "Aye-yah. Tis beautiful, but some o' the beads fell off whilst the dress was in the hope chest. Mum and I need ta be sewing 'em back on. Ya know, I'm really hopin' ta someday pass it on ta me own daughter someday. O' course, with the luck I have, I'll be havin' a bunch o' boys!"

I laughed. "Oh, we're already talking about children, are we?"

"Not too soon," she said. "But I'm hopin' ta have a dozen."

"A dozen? Don't come ask me to babysit!" I laughed at the thought of her sitting with a dozen kids on a front porch.

"I'll help you baby-sit," came the voice from behind me. Even before I turned around, I knew it was Harold. He'd been hanging around me whenever he could. He was so annoying. Even though he supposedly disliked Irish people, he was still coming around and talking with me, then he would tell Mrs. Fredericks I'd been the one flirting with him! I tried to ignore him when I could, but sometimes he'd try to get me in trouble in other ways if I did.

"There'll be no babysittin' fer a while, so go away," Anna snapped. "What're ya doin' outside anyway? Why aren't ya inside kissin' up ta the boss?"

"Very funny," he retorted. "At least I'm not outside playing all the time. Beth, I brought some apple pie with me today, and I thought you might want some of it."

"That's nice of you, Harold," I told him, "but I've had enough to eat. Thank you. Maybe we could share some later, at the afternoon break."

He smiled. "Great. I'll see you then." Then he leaned down close like he was going to whisper something to me, but he said in a clear, firm voice for Anna to hear, "See if you can leave her working at the vat." He winked at me and left.

"That boy is so irritating," I said.

"Then why on earth did ya tell him ya'd be splittin' that pie with him this afternoon?" she asked.

"Oh, basically to get rid of him. I'll come up with some excuse not to see him later."

"Next time, ya should just tell him ta go his way an' leave ya alone."

I grinned. "I wish I was brave enough to do that, but I don't like to cause any trouble."

"Ya'd best be getting' prickly, girl."

"Why?"

"'Cause ya can be certain that he likes ya, Beth." Then she added, "Ya poor dearie!"

"Oh, he's such a goon! Do you really think he likes me?" I made a face, and that made Anna laugh.

It was just about time for the whistle to signal the end of lunch when Anna saw a car coming around the corner. It was a big black Model T with a man and woman riding in it. As they came closer, Anna nudged me on the arm. "That couple seems a bit familiar ta me. Do ya know them?"

I looked closely, and I realized that I did know the couple in the car. The girl was Sadie Moore. The man driving was Tommy Viosca. My heart began to hurt.

"That's the boy you met at the Fourth of July picnic. You know, the boy I like. Tommy."

"An' who's that sittin' in the car with him? Is she that awful bird Sadie?"

"Yes."

"I can'nat believe it," Anna said with a groan. "That's crazy! Whate'er could the lad be seein' in her? She's got some cheek, makin' an absolute ninny o' herself when she's 'round him. Hrmph, she's so obvious."

"Maybe she is," I said, my voice wavering, "but she has Tommy."

We watched the car disappear down the street. After a long silence, she said, "Well, ya can always be takin' Harold."

I knew she was trying to make a joke, but I almost burst into tears. Anna came over to me and put her arms around me. "I didn'nat mean it!" she cried in mock horror. "I said ya could take him, but I didn'nat mean ya had ta be kapein' him! I was actually thinkin' we could throw him inta a river."

This time, I did laugh, a little bit. Then I said, "I'm sorry. It's just that I feel the same way about her that you do. I know she's wrong to throw herself at Tommy that way, yet she is with him and I'm stuck with Harold. I've a bad feeling about this whole thing."

"I'm so sorry." It was all she could say.

I pouted all the way back to the vats. For the next hour, all I could think about was Sadie sitting in the car with Tommy; her blond curls bouncing and her blue eyes lit up as she chatted on, probably about something meaningless and stupid.

Suddenly, Anna put her hands on her hips. "I know what ya be needin', lassie," she said. "Ya need ta take a night out ta go see the gypsies."

"The gypsies?" I gasped. "But Mum wouldn't allow me to go see them. Every year, when they come to town, I hear about them being here, but have never seen them. Unless they're on their way to the store or something. Mum says they can't be trusted."

"Tis but a myth. Aye-yah, maybe there're some o' the men who've stolen before, but that's a wee lot. Besides, I wasn'nat planning on ya spillin' everythin' ta yer mum. Me own parents wouldn'nat allow me ta go see them either, I'd wager, even bein' 18 now an' all. Perhaps we should go out an' have a look-see ourselves. Besides, bring yerself a nickel, and we'll have yer fortune told."

I gasped. "But isn't that of the devil?"

"Nay, it's just fer the fun o' it. Ya'll see."

We got back to work, and were chatting, when Mrs. Fredericks bustled by looking for some missing papers yet again. Anna rolled her eyes and twirled a finger near her temple, and I couldn't help but giggle. Even though we were no longer playing pranks on our boss, she still continued to lose things fairly often, all by herself.

Later that night, I found myself climbing out of my window and praying Mum wouldn't have any reason to come looking for me. Since I'd started working, she usually allowed me to sleep in late on Saturday mornings, and I didn't think she'd need me during the night. So, I climbed out and crawled down the tree next to my bedroom window. Anna was waiting for me at the edge of the backyard. The neighborhood dogs barked some, but they didn't make any more noise than usual.

We didn't talk at all, until we got a couple of blocks away. Then I asked her, "Have you ever seen them before?"

"Aye-yah," she said. "I've even been gettin' ta know some o' them. They're just regular folk, like me an' ya. They even came from another country, just as me an' mine did. I don't know which country, mind ya, but they're all wearin' bright colors, an' the lasses wear bands an' bands of gold bracelets an' earrings. Even some o' the men wear earrings!"

I gasped. "Really? Men with earrings?"

"Aye-yah! An' they travel 'round in beautifully painted carts, or in wagons. This depression has hit them as hard as the rest o' us. Most are decent, honest folk just tryin' ta make ends meet by helpin' out at farms."

"And telling fortunes?"

She grinned. "Aye-yah, they do that, too, but 'tis only fer fun. Did ya bring yer nickel?" I assured her that I had. "They'll also be playin' instruments. Ya know, banjos, guitars, an' the like. They're really good."

"Are they nice people?"

"I'd say so. Leastwise, they're nicer than auld Harold."

"Ha ha, very funny," I told her, irritated at the thought of him. Thankfully, he never did come around that afternoon to share the pie he'd offered.

Quietly, we made our way to the edge of some woods. The moon was bright, and we could see a bonfire in the distance.

"Look yonder! There they'd be," she pointed out. There was a band of gypsies, sitting out in the warm summer night, playing instruments and dancing. A small crowd of people had gathered to watch.

In the middle of the dancers, there was a young man, probably only a little older than me. His dark hair was wavy, and his skin was olive, like mine. Dark eyes peered out at the crowd. Muscular and tall, he wore a long-sleeved shirt with gray and red pants and a matching vest. He was dancing some sort of sword dance that I had never seen before. As we came closer, the music grew louder and the young man danced faster.

"He's cute. He's got gorgeous eyes," I whispered to her.

"That he does. But are they more gorgeous than yer Tommy's?"

"If Tommy ever looks at me, I'll let you know," I said sarcastically. Anna giggled at that. We watched and watched, wide eyed, as the music swelled and the pace increased. The young man danced, twisted, and twirled over the swords that were lying on the ground. I looked closely and noticed that Anna had been right about the men wearing earrings. Even so, he was quite attractive.

Suddenly, the music stopped. He came to a halt and threw up his arms. The crowd applauded wildly, and he bowed. When he looked up, our eyes met. I could feel myself blush, so I turned away. When I snuck a peek at him, he grinned at me.

Some softer music began, and a girl appeared. She must've been older than me, I thought, because she was much prettier than I could ever hope to be. Her hair was long and as black as mine, but it was straight with a thread of gold fabric woven through the long ponytail in back. Her eyes were wide and brown, but they held a hint of mystery and sadness that I can't properly describe. She was wearing a beautiful red skirt with a matching sash around her white blouse. Large gold earrings adorned her ears, and gold bracelets hung on her arm, just as Anna had said. She started dancing slowly, in a way that reminded me of ballet. Her bare feet moved gracefully along with the music, then picked up speed as the music did. Before I knew it, she had the entire crowd cheering and she went and flirted with the old men who threw some coins at her feet. She would kiss one on the cheek and then go flirt with another.

"I wish I could dance like that," I told Anna.

"I'm certain ya could," she answered, "but I'm not sure ya'd be wantin' ta. She dances fer coins, but in some gypsy bands, the lasses are asked ta take off some o' their clothes."

"You're kidding!" I inhaled sharply. I couldn't imagine men staring at me while I undressed. The thought made me shudder.

Several minutes later, a man somewhere in the crowd screamed, "Take it off!"

"Yeah, honey," shouted another one. "Let's see some skin!"

I watched as the girl continued to dance, but she never lost her smile. I felt sorry for her, but the good-looking male dancer walked over to the two men and told them to leave. I couldn't see if they did, but the girl continued to dance and to flirt with the rest of the crowd.

"'Tis so grand!" Anna said. "Look at the way they're dancin'. They're so full o' life. That's what I'm wantin', ta enjoy me life."

"How do you know so much about these gypsies?" I asked, watching as the celebration became more and more lively.

"I told ya, I've met some o' them," she said. "After all, they've been comin' here fer years. This band is just a bunch o' hard-workin' field hands. They're good folk."

Knowing that, I felt a little more at ease. We watched as the people finished up their dancing, then we went in search of the fortune teller. An eerie feeling coursed through me as we knocked on the door of the old woman's wagon.

"Who is it?" came a voice from inside.

"We'd like to find out our fortunes," Anna answered. She called for us to come in, but I wasn't about to go in until Anna did. I held her hand and followed.

From behind a beaded curtain, the ancient woman called for us to sit down at the table. "Pour yourself a cup of tea, my dears," her worn voice called out to us. "Madame will be with you shortly."

We sat at a round table, and I stared at the ornamental rugs that hung from the walls. Sitting on the table were some china cups and a small pitcher of tea. I didn't want any, so I looked around at the old rugs again. The old woman appeared from behind the beaded curtain. "I am sorry to inconvenience you," she apologized, "but I am watching my grandchildren tonight, and they must get their rest. I am Madame Cazacu. Welcome."

Thinking of this old woman as a grandmother helped me feel more comfortable about talking with her. As she took her seat, she asked me why I hadn't drunk the tea she had prepared for me.

"Oh," I exclaimed. "No thank you, ma'am. I thought it was your tea."

Anna burst out laughing. "'Tis not fer her, Beth. 'Tis yer tea. She kapes it on the table so she can use it fer fortune-tellin'. Ya'll be needin' ta drink a cup o' tea."

"I thought that fortune tellers used a crystal ball?" I whispered.

She laughed again. "Nay, they read tea leaves from the bottom o' yer cup."

"Oh," I said, feeling rather embarrassed. Obediently, I poured my tea.

"So, do you live here in Allan County?" the old woman asked.

"I do," I said. "I grew up here, but Anna was born in Ireland."

"I see," she said. "So you are friends, not sisters."

"Ye're correct," Anna said. "We met at the place where we're workin'."

"Work?"

"Yes," I explained, "We work at the Hillerman Chicken Factory."

We talked a while about the factory, our families, and even what I wanted to do when I grew up. I was happy to find that she was a very pleasant person.

"Now, young one," she said, "let me see your cup, and I will tell you your fortune." I handed her the cup and watched as she examined the bottom carefully. To my surprise, she started telling me about some of the people I work with.

"There is a young man, no? I do not see his name, but he works with you, and he has set his cap for you, yes?"

"Well, yes!" I blurted out. "She's talking about Harold!" I said excitedly to Anna.

"And there is another worker there, one who is mean, yes? Is that your boss?"

"Oh, golly! Yes! The boss lady is very rude. Her name is Mrs. Fredericks. And Mr. Reed is much worse than she is."

"Oh, I see problems with them," she told me. "Keep away from them when they are together. One is bad enough, but do not be with both of them. Together, they will be dangerous for you." I stared at Anna.

For several minutes, she told me things about my work and family, so I couldn't help but ask her if I would ever be able to return to school.

"Hmm," she mused, staring at the cup again. "At this time, I would say yes, you will return to school, where I suspect there is a boy who is your true love. But first you must live through a winter of sorrow. In the spring, you must find the courage to do what you must, then it will be time for you to go back. That is all I can tell you. Madame C has spoken." Then she reached down under the table and found a fan to cool herself.

I didn't know what to do, so I sat there for a moment, staring at her. Anna stood up from her chair and told the old woman thank you. I stood up, too, and gave her my thanks as well. "I appreciate your time," I told her.

"Give her the nickel," Anna hissed under her breath.

"Oh, yes. Here's a nickel." I laid it on the table and thanked her again. We turned to leave, and I asked Anna if she was going to have her fortune told as well.

"Nay," she said with a gracious smile. "I'm ta be gettin' married, so I'm already knowin' how good me fortune is."

"Congratulations," the older woman said. "I wish you the best of luck and blessings."

"Thank ya," she said, and we left the wagon. As we started home, I asked Anna how the woman had done that.

"Can ya not see it? When she got ya ta talkin' about yerself, she found the tips on what ta be sayin'. When ye mentioned workin' at the fact'ry, she knew there was ta be at least one boss who was mean. Ya were the one who added the names."

"Oh," I said. "But wait a minute. How did she know about Harold? He has 'set his cap' for me, but I really want to be with Tommy."

"Twas simple. Yer a pretty lass, and yer young and pleasant, so she was figurin' there must be a boy 'round ya. If ya hadn't mentioned Harold's name, she'd be sayin' 'twas a secret admirer instead, as everyone likes a wee bit o' romance."

"Then how did she know about Tommy?" I pressed on.

"Twas easy. When ya said, 'She's talkin' 'bout Harold,' ya said his name in such a way that anyone could tell yer not in love with him."

"Well, that's whacky," I said incredulously, "She was good!"

We continued a long way before I said, "That was kind of fun. She had me convinced that she knew all about me, just from looking at my teacup! Maybe I should've asked her if I had any chance with Tommy, or if he really likes Sadie Moore better," I said, remembering the scene from earlier that day.

"Well," Anna said calmly, "it's best ya remember that 'twas just fer fun. She couldn'na told ya if he really loves the lass or not."

"Yes, I guess that is true. But it was worth a shot."

We ran along the dark streets of the township, and I told Anna good-bye at the end of my block. I snuck back into the house through the back door, and tip-toed down the hallway. Mum and Papa were still snoring away in bed, so I went to my room and changed into my bedclothes. The bed was warm, and the winds blowing through the open window were cool. I snuggled down under my covers, and was just about to drift off to sleep, when something strange dawned on me.

The gypsy lady had tricked me into talking about myself so she could tell my fortune. But how had she come to the conclusion that the oncoming winter was to be one filled with sorrow? And were Mr. Reed and Mrs. Fredericks really dangerous when they were together? What about that? And what did she mean by saying that I had to have courage?

It took me a long time to fall asleep.

CHAPTER TEN
An Unexpected Trip

Within a couple of weeks, the October winds made the morning walks to the factory quite chilly. By noon, things would warm up, but then the sun would set almost immediately after work and it would get cooler again. As I was getting dressed one morning, I came across a dress Mum had made for me last year. It had a nice warm jacket that I could take off if I got hot, so I thought it would be perfect with the crazy weather.

But as I was putting it on, my sleeve somehow got twisted. I was struggling to fix it when Mum walked past my door and saw my predicament.

"Here, let me help ya," she said

"Thanks, Mum." I freed my hand as she straightened out the sleeve and helped me into the jacket. I turned around to thank her, but the look on her face wasn't good.

"Mercy me!" she gasped. "Beth, look at how much weight ya've lost!"

I turned back to the mirror. She was right, I suppose. I had lost some weight, but I didn't think it was anything to worry about. It had been a long, hot summer, and I was never very hungry after working in the factory heat all day. To make matters worse, I couldn't really eat when Mum was worried, and she was always worried. She often fretted over bills or the fact Dale hadn't written, and now she was fretting over my weight.

She made me eat a large breakfast that morning, and then she fussed at me all the way to work, but I didn't mind. At least she was noticing me.

We got to the factory just as the whistle blew and the gates were opened. I was actually in a pretty good mood when I headed for the lockers and grabbed my boots, but before I could get them on, Mrs. Fredericks appeared out of nowhere.

"Mrs. Sundo, Elizabeth. I need to see both of you in my office." That was it. No "please" or anything. She just stared at us.

I looked at Anna, and she silently mouthed, "It'll be ok," but I could tell she was worried as well. Had she figured out that it was Anna and me who pulled all those pranks? Why did she need Mum?

I put my stuff away and followed her and Mum into the office. She took a seat at her desk and peered at me over the top of her glasses. I hated it when she did that; it was like she thought she was better than me or something.

"Mrs. Sundo," she began, turning her gaze towards Mum and ignoring me totally, "It would seem there is a problem with your daughter's employment with the Hillerman Chicken Factory. It has come to my attention that she is only 14 years old, not 15 as you have suggested."

In that moment, my thoughts raced into three different directions. Part of me felt my stomach knot up, knowing we were caught and afraid we'd both be fired. Then there was the part of me that was terrified and wanted desperately to stay and work just so we'd have a house to live in and I could continue being friends with Anna.

But the third thought, assuming Mum didn't lose her job as well, was the hope that I would be fired and forced to go back to school. There was so much joy at that thought that I felt a little over-whelmed. Being forced to go to school, to see my friends again, and to have time to read books and practice writing like a newspaper reporter? That would have been a dream come true!

"Please, please please," I thought to myself, "let them fire me and keep Mum."

"Mrs. Sundo, we at the Hillerman Chicken factory cannot afford for anyone from the government to come in here and find children working on the lines. If these new child labor laws or those Federal Work Laws are implemented, we could be heavily fined, and that could mean that you lose your job, and many others could lose theirs as well."

"What does that mean?" I asked.

"It means that if the government passes these laws, we'd have to pay money fer not following them," Mum explained.

"She will not be allowed to return to work until she is 15. Is that clear?" Mrs. Fredericks was only looking at Mum, still ignoring me completely.

"Aye-yah, ma'am," Mum told her with her usual grace and dignity. "That's only a few weeks away. She'll be returning ta her work after that."

"If we still have an opening," Mrs. Fredericks told her.

"She'll be back," Mum said with emphasis. "Good day, Mrs. Fredericks." And with that, she stood up and held her head high. "Come along, me dear.'

I followed her out of the office in a tangled mess of feelings. On the one hand, I definitely didn't want to be there in the first place, but on the other hand, no one wants to be fired from their first job, either. I guess I would feel… I don't know… humiliated? It would give Mrs. Fredericks and people like her even more reason to look down on me.

But I was disappointed, too. And a little angry. Mum had said I would be returning after my birthday. I didn't want to return. I wanted to go back to school.

But sometimes I guess you have to accept things the way they are. I tried to find a bright side, and all I could think was, "Oh, well, at least I'll have a month off for a vacation."

"I know Mr. Reed knows yer not 15; so does Mrs. Fredericks," Mum was saying in a gentle voice, like she was trying to cheer me up or something. "Happens all the time. The only reason they care right now is because they don't want ta get in trouble with the inspectors when they come in a couple of weeks.

"Besides, I wouldn't worry. It's only for a few weeks, just until yer birthday. I got a letter the other day from me Da, yer Grandpap O'Brien. He said that all of yer cousins are coming ta the farm ta help out with the last of the harvesting, and he wanted ta know if ya and Dale could help out. I was going ta write and tell them ya couldn't, but now that yer out of work, ya can go and take Denny with ya. He was invited ta go along, too."

"What?"

"Sure, ya can go help yer grandparents for a month. Won't that be fun?"

Well, so much for a month-long vacation.

I wanted to tell Mum I would rather stay home and help her. I started to tell her that I wasn't all that excited about having to put up with Denny on a long trip, either. There were a lot of things I wanted to tell her, but as usual, I kept my mouth shut.

"What happened?" Anna asked when I got back to the vats. "What was she sayin'?"

"I'm too young to work here," I said in a voice mimicking Mrs. Fredericks. I put on my coat and got ready to leave.

"I wouldn'nat be worryin' about it," Anna laughed. "Tis nothing ta do with ya. There'll be some folks from the government comin' fer a tour. Once they're gone, ya kin come back."

"Mum said the same thing. Well, I'll see you in a month."

"Beth, ya can come up here someday an' have lunch with me. They'll let ya on the property. An' I can come ta visit ya."

"No, you can't," I told her sadly. "I won't be here. I'll be at my Grandpap's farm in York."

Then something happened that I never thought I'd see. Anna's eyes teared up. "Ya will? But, but ya will be back fer me weddin', won't ya?"

"I'll only be gone for a month," I said with a hug. "I promise. My mum already told Mrs. Fredericks that I would be back next month."

"Tis a relief then," she said. "I'll be missin' ya. Ya'd best be hurryin' back."

It was funny. I'd never seen Anna anything but brave and strong, yet here she was, tearing up because she'd be missing me. That's when I knew she'd be the best friend I'd ever have.

"After all," she added, suddenly returning to her old, wise-cracking self, "I'm sure Harold will be missin' ya, too."

"Aw, get on with yourself. If you keep threatening me like that, I'm definitely not coming back," I told her, making both of us laugh.

Two days later, I found myself meeting Aunt Martha and Dennis at the train station. It was barely daylight, and Dennis was already jumping up and down saying, "Is it time yet? I've never ridden on a train before!"

"Didn't yer mother come with ya, me dear?" Aunt Martha asked.

"No, ma'am," I griped. "Mrs. Fredericks wouldn't let Mum off work long enough to come to the station with me, but Papa's here. He's over there buying the tickets."

"Oh, well, I'm so sorry about that," she said. "I've made a wonderful lunch fer ya and Denny, but mind ya don't let him eat his pie until he's eaten his sandwich and fruit."

"Aw, Mum," Denny complained. "I know I'm supposed to eat my sandwich first. I'm not a little kid, ya know."

I laughed. Denny was only 7.

"I promise to take care of him for you," I told her.

"Thank you. I also put some books in the basket fer ya. They're some novels we had at the store. Take good care of them because I can still sell them after ya are finished reading them."

"Thanks!" I said as I thumbed through them.

"Here are the tickets," Papa said. "Good morning, Martha. How are you doing?"

"I'm fine now, knowing that Dennis will be travelling with Beth makes me feel a lot better."

We heard the porter call for everyone to go aboard, so Papa gave me a hug and Aunt Martha hugged us both.

"Now you listen to Beth, and behave for your grandparents, understand?" she told Denny.

He rolled his eyes. "Yes, ma'am," he said, and we climbed the steps to the train.

Then she turned to me and said, "Hug me Mum and Da, and tell them how much yer mother and I miss them, all right?"

"Sure thing," I said with a chuckle. "Mum told me to tell them the same thing!"

We boarded and found our seats quickly, but there was still a five-minute wait before the train started. I could see Papa and Aunt Martha standing next to the ticket office, talking. As soon as we heard the whistle and felt the train pull forward, Denny and I both jumped up and started waving at them through the window. They looked up and waved back, and I watched the station growing smaller in the distance.

Denny was excited. He was already chatting away. "I can't wait to see Grandma and Grandpap again," he said. "I want to see my cousins again, too. I haven't seen Fred in a long time, and I have new toy cowboys and horses I want to show him. I also like reading stories about cowboys and the West and stuff, and maybe you can read some to me at night before bedtime. I hope you like to read. Can I have an apple?"

He was so annoying and so cute at the same time.

I dug in the basket and tossed him an apple. "Here you go."

He chatted on for the most part of an hour. I had tried reading one of the dime-store novels Aunt Martha had loaned me, but Dennis squirmed and fidgeted so much it was difficult. When I finally got him to read one of his books about western cowboys, it kept him quiet long enough to let me read some, too.

I didn't realize how much time had passed when I looked up and saw that we were no longer in the city. We were passing through some trees thick enough I had to stare hard to see anything else. I could see an occasional field or a church steeple in the distance. Not much else, though, so I went back to reading.

"Wow!" I heard Denny exclaim a little while later. "That looks like fun! I want to go camping sometime!"

I turned to see what he was talking about, and realized we'd passed a couple of campsites, but not regular campsites. Hoovervilles, they were called, after former President Hoover. I'd heard of those, and even seen pictures of some in the newspapers, but these were real, and right in front of me. There were rows of houses made out of boxes, sheets of tin, old tires, and some that looked like they were made from nothing more than poles and old blankets.

There were a few adults walking around, mostly women, cleaning clothes in a boiling pot and cooking lunch on open fires. But what I really noticed was the number of children I saw. They looked like they were also working on chores, stopping long enough to watch the train pass. Some had shoes, some didn't. Some were white, others were black. None looked like they'd had very much to eat in a while.

I looked down at the basket of food Aunt Martha had given me, and looked around at the seats we were in. The smell of coffee that the porters were making for passengers hung in the air. I looked back to the children and the sad situation. I didn't tell Denny that those people weren't camping by choice. They weren't going to a nice warm home at the end of their "camping trips."

"Here," I told him instead. "It's time for lunch. Take your sandwich."

By this time, the Hooverville was disappearing into the distance, and Denny was willing to settle back down and eat. There was a thermos of milk he and I split, but other than that, I didn't eat much. I tore off a couple of pieces of bread from one of the sandwiches and nibbled on them. Thinking of all those children made me lose my appetite.

Where were the men? I kept wondering. I'd seen mostly women and children at that camp, but hardly any men. Where were they? Why weren't they taking care of their families? Were they at work? I couldn't imagine many of them had jobs, living this far out of town. Thinking about it made me irritable.

Denny finished his lunch and ate some of his pie, then he dutifully cleaned up after himself and set about to reading again, but the full feeling and the warm sunshine made him fall asleep in his chair. I thought that was the perfect time to read one of my own books, but I must have dozed off a bit, too.

Suddenly, the train stopped, jerking me awake. I didn't even realize I'd nodded off until that moment. Looking out my window, I knew we weren't at the station. A sense of confusion loomed in the train car. Others were standing up, looking out the windows to see why we'd stopped.

Outside, I could see another little shanty town in the distance, but this one was different from the last one. Rows of abandoned houses, boarded up, barely hanging together.

Then I noticed there were lights in some of the windows and smoke from several of the chimneys. That's when I knew people were living in them.

Then I saw what the other passengers had seen earlier. Police were chasing a couple of men away from the train. For a few moments, I was afraid, but then I realized they weren't trying to hurt those of us on board; they were just a couple of poor souls who wanted to catch a ride. After a few moments, they all disappeared, and the train started again.

Fortunately, Denny slept through the whole thing.

For the next hour, I contemplated the scene I'd witnessed. I thought about the stores that were shut down and empty. Sad dreams, boarded up, someone's life shut down. Broken windows, broken lives, shattered glass and shattered dreams. The whole thing broke my heart.

Then I began thinking about Dale. The night he left, did he catch a train, like these men had tried to do? Was he living in dilapidated buildings that had been abandoned years earlier? Why didn't he come home?

I was still angry with him for leaving us like that. If he was living in conditions like that, maybe he deserved it. He'd be in our nice warm home if he hadn't left. It put me in a bad mood, so I was glad Denny missed it.

By the time he woke up, I'd calmed down a lot, and we were almost to our station.

CHAPTER ELEVEN

The O'Brien Farm

I spotted him the second we got off the train. "Grandpap!" We ran and hugged him, and I couldn't help but look around for Grandma.

"Yer grandmother's at the house," he said, knowing who I was looking for. "She's makin' dinner fer everyone. We've pretty much all the grandkids here, ya know. Everyone 7 and up is here ta help out."

Then he looked over at me. "I hear we 'most didn'nat get a visit from ya, little lassie, since yer a workin' girl and all now," he continued, beaming like he was proud of me or something.

I was a little embarrassed by the remark. I don't know why. It's an honorable job and everything, but I still hated the fact people knew I was working there. Perhaps it was because I was more embarrassed about not being in school. Worse than that, I didn't really want to be working on the farm, either, but I couldn't tell anyone that, especially my own grandpap.

"Well, now I guess I'll be working with you," I said with a forced smile.

My cousin, Merle, had been standing quietly near the truck. With a quick hello, he came over and grabbed our things and headed back to the truck. He and Denny crawled into the back with the luggage, and I took a seat up front with Grandpap. It wasn't a long drive, and we were so busy talking that the ride was over in no time.

When we arrived, it did seem like everyone was there. Grandma and Grandpap, of course, plus two aunts and two uncles. There were also cousins I knew well, and cousins I hadn't seen since they were babies. Fred and Lila were the two youngest, and they were a year or so younger than Denny. Merle was the oldest, and like me, he'd be going back to work after the harvest was brought in. There were five other cousins between Merle's age and the little ones. With Denny and me joining them, there was a total of sixteen people around the dinner table that night.

It was a lot of fun, seeing everyone there, and we had a little reunion party. We ate chicken and dumplings, and Grandma made cake for dessert. After dinner, we cleaned the dishes while Grandpap played the fiddle that he'd brought with him when he first came to America. Even though I hated washing dishes, there were so many of us laughing and talking that it was fun. Before long, though, we had to go to bed, because the next few days would be long ones.

Early the next morning, when Grandma woke me up, she asked me to help with breakfast.

"Sure," I told her in a haze. I wasn't fully recovered from the long train ride, but I certainly didn't mind helping. I was thrilled, thinking I'd much rather help Grandma with the cooking than to be in the hot fields all day.

I dressed quickly, then helped her get the eggs from the chickens, slice up some ham and toast some bread.

But I was mistaken to think I'd be there to help her in the kitchen all day.

Once the whole family was around the table for breakfast, everyone was chatting away and Aunt Ida said, "By the way, Beth, I'll need ya ta come back from the fields around eleven o'clock."

I sat, motionless. "Ma'am?" I ventured.

"I said I'll need to see ya in here early, so you can help us carry lunches back out ta the fields." She chatted happily away as my heart sank. I'd hoped to stay with Grandma and help her out. Not so much because it would be easier work, which it would be, but more so because I wanted to spend time with her. I'd dreamed how it would be just me in her, in the kitchen, talking and cooking together.

Silently, I ate my eggs.

We headed out to the fields just as the sun was rising. My job for that day was to get the cucumbers. I grabbed a basket and went to the family vegetable garden while everyone else went on to the main fields.

I'd been in Grandma's little garden before, usually in the summertime when the flowers were in bloom and the aroma was so sweet you would have thought she used sugar instead of dirt. Just beyond that garden was the vegetable garden where she'd planted stuff she would use for the family and not for sales. But today, in October, it was dreary and cool, and the flowers in the garden had already crumpled and fallen away. The vegetables were ready, but I'd been sent there alone. Great, I thought. Not only do I get to pull double duty in the kitchen and the garden, but I didn't even get to be out with everyone else.

I worked as fast as I could, hoping to be able to at least be with everyone else by the afternoon. I had to bend over a lot to get them, so eventually chose to kneel down and get my knees dirty. It took a little longer, but my back didn't hurt as much.

Finally, that was finished, and I returned to the house. I helped the adult women set up lunch, then I went back to the fields with everyone else. The day was long and warm, and my back was still hurting. We finally stopped about the time the sun set. I was thrilled to be able to go back inside.

Wow. And I thought working at the factory was hard!

Dinner was simpler than it had been the night before. Grandma made ham and beans and cornbread. While we ate, I looked around at the number of dishes that would need to be washed after dinner. I was so tired, and I didn't feel like helping with the dishes, but I chose to do what I normally do when I get frustrated; I didn't say anything.

"Beth, I need ya to grab the rest of the cornbread, wrap it up, and put it in tha breadbox fer me," Aunt Ida said. "And then I need ya ta…"

"Actually, Ida," Grandpap broke in, "I believe Beth's a wee bit sacked. She was the first one up ta help ya this morning, and she worked in tha kitchen durin' the noon meal and helped with the wee ones. I think she could use a bit o' kip."

I could have jumped up and hugged him.

"But Da," Ida complained, "I think she's old enough to help out more than the younger children."

"And she has done that," he said.

"Ida," Grandma said with a sternness in her voice I'd never heard before. "Yer da is right. The girl needs a rest. The younger children know how ta clean plates as sound as anyone else in this family. They can help. If everyone washes their own dishes, it won't take much time fer us ta clean up."

Aunt Ida gave me a stern look, then her eyes softened, and her frown faded into a smile. "Oh, get along and get your rest," she said.

I ran in and hugged Grandma tightly. "Thank you," I whispered, then I hugged Grandpap. I quickly washed my plate, and I was done for the day. I went into the sitting room and curled up near a window to read my book. Grandpap came in as well, playing his violin again, and eventually the whole family joined us in the room.

Once everyone had cleaned the dishes and the little ones were ready for bed, Grandma read to us from the Bible, then we all joined hands while Grandpap said a prayer, and it was off to bed.

That's how almost every day went while we were on the farm. I helped with breakfast, worked in the fields, helped with lunch, worked a little more in the fields, and helped get the little ones cleaned up for dinner. Grandma and Grandpap insisted that as long as I was helping prepare meals, I didn't have to clean up after dinner.

The evenings became my favorite time of the day. I would often sit in the sitting room, or if it was too warm inside, we'd go out to the porch. We talked, read books, or listened to Grandpap play his fiddle.

One evening, I was writing a letter to Anna at a desk in the sitting room when I noticed Denny, Fred, and Lila in a corner, whispering about something. Over and over again they counted, but I couldn't quite figure out what they were up to.

"Grandpap," Lila said, "if we found a baby donkey, could we keep it at the farm?"

"Well, I'm supposin' ya could, but I'm thinkin' ya'll not be findin' any baby donkeys 'round here. And even if ya did, we'd need ta be ta see if any of the neighbors had lost a wee donkey."

"But if we bought it, could we keep it?" Fred asked.

"If we used our own money," Denny reasoned with him, "it'd be ours and no one else could take it from us, right?"

"If ya paid fer it, I don'na see why ya couldn'at kape it," Grandpap answered. "But how do ya s'pose the three of ya ta be payin' fer a baby donkey?"

"We got a secret!" Fred told him.

"Yeah!" the others chimed in.

Grandpap rubbed his chin, but he gave up and went back to reading his paper. I didn't really think too much about the conversation at the time, but the next day I found out why they were asking about donkeys.

"Beth, Beth!" Denny called as he came running up to me the next day, holding something in his hands. Fred and Lila were right behind him, screaming for Grandpap to come see what they had.

"What is it?" I asked.

"It's a donkey egg!" they squealed. "Grandpap! Come see our donkey egg!"

"A what?" I couldn't believe it.

"What's this?" Grandpap asked as he walked up.

"It's our donkey egg!" they all said as Denny proudly presented Grandpap with their prized egg. I took one look at it and began laughing. Grandpap chuckled.

Nestled in Denny's little hands was a coconut.

"Now, now, Beth," Grandpap gently chastised, "I don'nat guess ya should be laughing. After all, 'tis brown and furry, just like a donkey."

"And it is small and round," I added.

"And when it hatches, we get to keep the baby donkey that's inside it!" Lila said. "You said we could keep it here, right?"

"Well, I'm not one ta be goin' back on a promise," he said gently. "Where did ya get this here egg?"

"From Merle," they all said in unison. "We bought it from him for twelve cents," Denny added proudly.

I laughed even harder. I have no idea where Merle would've found a coconut, especially in Pennsylvania, and in the fall, but he did.

"What's wrong?" Denny asked.

I hugged him and left Grandpap to explain to them about coconuts. Even though I felt really bad for them, I couldn't stop laughing and thought it was best to leave.

The kids were disappointed about the baby donkey, but Grandpap made Merle give the money back. And since they still got to keep the coconut, they were happy.

A week later, I discovered where Merle got his talent for playing tricks on people, and I learned the hard way. He got it from Grandpap! Merle seemed like a beginner next to him.

Somehow, the dinner conversation had turned to funny things that Grandpap did when he was growing up, then the funny pranks he pulled on my aunts and uncles when they were kids. Everyone was telling stories and we were laughing so much my cheeks began to ache and my eyes had grown watery. Of course, I didn't want to miss a single story, so I even stayed in the kitchen area and helped with the dishes for a bit before Grandpap and my uncles went to relax in the sitting room.

"Grandpap," I whispered excitedly, sitting on the footstool next to him. "I pulled a prank on someone once, too."

His eyes twinkled. "What did ya do?"

I told him about the time Anna and I got Mrs. Fredericks to douse herself with the water in her own teacup, and he laughed.

"Sure an' I ought ta try that sometime meself," he said. "Hey! I've an idea! Why don't ya an' I try gettin' Merle with that one? After all, he needs some payback fer the donkey egg incident."

I couldn't help but to be flattered that Grandpap thought I could help out on one of his tricks. Immediately, I agreed to help. "What do you need me to do?"

"I can get yer grandma in here, and ya be fetchin' her fav'rite cup, put the water in it, and put it high upon the shelf. Then, we'll ask Merle ta fetch it down fer her. He wouldn'nat think twice 'bout gettin' something fer his own grandmother. 'Twill be easy."

"All right," I said as I stood up.

"Mary," he called, winking at me, "could ya come in here fer a moment?"

As Grandma came into the room, I was already on my way into the kitchen in search of the beloved cup. I had to hurry to get the water in it and hide it, but I got done just in time for Grandma to return.

I wandered back into the sitting room, sat down next to Grandpap, and waited for him to call Merle into the room.

"Sweetheart," he called out, "Do ya have it? I can'nat fix it fi ya can'not bring it ta me."

"I almost have it," she called back. "But someone's put it way back near the back o' the cabinet. I can barely reach it."

It took me a second to realize what was going on. He hadn't talked Merle into getting the cup at all—he'd sent Grandma!

"No! Grandma, don't!" I yelled as I ran back into the kitchen, but it was too late. I arrived just in time to see her pull down the teacup sending the cold water down on top of her head. Her eyes grew large and her face reddened.

"What's the meanin' o' this? Who did this?"

"Oh, no, Grandma!" I squawked. "I'm sorry! It was supposed to be for Merle, to get him back for the donkey egg trick he played on the little ones!"

By this time, however, everyone in the house heard the commotion and came running to see what was happening. My poor grandmother stood with water dripping from her hair and face.

"Beth!" Grandpap yelled in a stern voice, "how could ya do that ta yer own, poor grandmother? Wait till I tell yer parents about this."

"But Grandma," I began pleading. "I didn't do it. I mean, I did, but it was Grandpap's idea. Really!"

"And to try ta blame yer own grandpap," Merle said. "Beth, I can't believe you just did that!"

"But," I started, and Grandpap and Merle practically fell down laughing. Then Grandma must have realized what had happened because she started laughing, too. Then we were all laughing, even me. And I thought how amusing it was that I now had my own story of being tricked by Grandpap.

CHAPTER TWELVE
Questions and Answers

Denny and I stayed with Grandma and Grandpap for three, nearly four weeks. On the last Sunday before we left, I was sitting at the kitchen table cutting up some potatoes to add to the stew for dinner that night. Everyone else was gone to a nearby farm to see a new baby calf and visit with the neighbors, leaving me alone with Grandma. It was finally just her and me alone, talking and cooking.

We talked about work, school, and farming, when Grandma suddenly sat down across from me and said, "Elizabeth, I want to know somethin'."

She'd used my full name. It must be something big. I put down the potatoes and the knife.

"Do ya know why yer brother left?"

I looked down at my hands. "Well, sort of."

She didn't say anything. She just looked at me, waiting.

"Basically, he left to find work," I told her.

"And he didn't think he could find work near ta yer home?"

"Well, actually, I think he may have gotten that idea from Papa."

She looked shocked. "Yer papa told him ta go find a job?"

"No, no, Grandma. Nothing like that. I just think he overheard Papa talking to Mum. Actually, I know he did."

Her eyes still held questions. "So what happened?"

I sighed and started cutting the potatoes while I talked.

"Well, it was late one night, and I was still sort of hungry, so I was sneaking down to get a slice of bread and some of the apple butter Aunt Martha had brought over. I really thought everyone would be asleep, so I didn't think anyone would mind, but then I saw Dale crouched down at the top of the stairs. When I asked him what he was doing, he shushed me, and I hate it when he does that."

I paused, remembering.

"Downstairs, we could hear Mum and Papa talking. Well, really, they were arguing. And you know them; they never argue."

She nodded.

"I couldn't quite tell what was going on at first, but I could hear Mum crying, and then she said, 'But what about the children?' and 'I don't want to end up like Mrs. Fitzgerald.' And that made Papa angry. He even yelled at her."

"What does that mean, about ending up like Mrs. Fitzgerald?" she interrupted.

"Well, Mrs. Fitzgerald is the lady who lived down the street from us. She was married, and they had three kids and a nice car. But after the stock market crashed, her husband left to find work, and no one's heard from him since. We've heard rumors that he went to live with another lady, or that he died or something, but no one knows for sure. He just vanished. After a while, she lost her house, and she sent her children out west to be adopted by strangers who could afford to feed them, and now she lives alone in her car. She works day jobs to pay for food and gasoline and stuff."

Just thinking of Mum being alone sent shivers through me, and we don't even have a car for her to live in. Tears started to rush into my eyes.

Grandma still looked perplexed. "Why did she think she'd end up like Mrs. Fitzgerald?"

"Because," I told her, "Papa was wanting to leave home to find work."

"Oh, no."

I began slicing some carrots. "Anyway, I was too upset to eat anything after that, so I went back to bed, but Dale was still at the top of the stairs when I left. I finally fell asleep, but then something woke me up. I didn't really think anything about it at the time, but I'd heard a noise, so I went to investigate."

Suddenly, I remembered a detail I hadn't thought of before. "When I didn't find anything, I went ahead and snuck a slice of bread and apple butter. But while I was in the kitchen, I looked out the window and saw someone running down the alley. At the time, I thought it was a bum rushing to catch a train because that happens all the time near our house. Now, though, I think it must have been Dale I saw running down the alley, because the next morning, Mum woke me up all panicked and asking if I knew where he was, but I didn't. Papa and Uncle Randall went looking for him, and Aunt Martha came over to stay with Mum because she was so distraught that Dr. Viosca had to come over and give her some sort of sedative, so she was in bed most of the day."

Then, my voice cracked a little while I tried not to cry. "Mum hasn't been her usual self since then. And I guess he found some work with the Civilian Conservation Corps because he sends us money from time to time, but that doesn't help her mood any.

"So basically, Dale left so Papa wouldn't have to, and Papa definitely won't leave now because he needs to be there to take care of Mum and me."

Grandma rested her chin in her hand, looking lost in thought. "Hmm… I suppose I can see his reasonin.' I think he'd rather see yer papa stayin' close ta home rather than him, and he is almost old enough ta be out on his own. I guess that makes sense. At least in his mind it does."

I grunted.

"So, how do ya feel about the whole thing? Are ya okay, Elizabeth?"

I was shocked. It was like the first time anyone had asked me about my feelings about what was going on with my life. I dropped what I was doing and started crying.

"Grandma, I hate it. Mum and Papa seem so worried about Dale that I'm almost invisible, and I hate, hate, hate working at the factory."

Then an avalanche of emotions came tumbling out of me. "The bosses are mean, and there's this guy named Harold that keeps bugging me and saying nasty things to me, but all the boss lady does is say, 'Boys will be boys; take it as a compliment,' and stuff like that. And I miss my friends, and I can't go to school, and I have to work twelve hours a day, and the water's cold, and my back aches, and Mr. Reed almost hit me once!"

By this time, she'd moved around the table and put her arms around me and just held me close while I sobbed and sobbed. I told her about Mr. Reed almost slapping me, about the crummy working conditions, how I'd cried the entire day when I realized I was missing the last day of school. I went on and on.

"Grandma, I don't want to work in a chicken factory all my life. I want to be a writer. I want to be a newspaper reporter, and I can't do that at a factory."

She unwrapped her arms and gently grabbed my face and wiped away my tears. "Lass, someday, ya will be a writer. And I know ya will," she said, looking deeply into my eyes. "You were made for so much more than this. You were born ta write. Aye-yah, maybe right now yer havin' ta work at that factory, but someday, this will end, and ya can go back ta school, and maybe even college. Who knows? But ya won't be in that factory forever. *You* are too smart fer a place like that. Ya have too much talent, and I believe in ya."

Other than my English teacher, Mr. Bedgood, I don't think I'd ever heard anyone say anything like that to me.

"Really? You think I can do it?"

"Really. I think ya *will* do it. I've seen yer talent."

"You have?" I was shocked.

"Aye-yah. I've seen it in the letters ya've sent me. And ya might be a bit shy, but ya have spirit. And ye're smart, and ya are going ta make yerself a wonderful life. After all, ya are me own granddaughter, aren't ya?"

A small smile appeared. I couldn't think of a better compliment. "Yes."

She grabbed a towel from her apron pocket and wiped my face. "Now, let's focus on somethin' happy. The others will be back soon, and I need ta be finishin' the stew. So let's focus on somethin' positive. Tell me about just one good thing in yer life."

"Well," I sniffled. "The only good thing is my friend Anna."

She smiled and then went back to the stove, taking the cut-up carrots and potatoes with her. I told her all about Anna, and how she looked, and how funny she was, and how we both disliked Sadie Moore. I even told her about the gypsies, but I didn't tell her the part where I snuck out of the house without telling Mum. We talked and laughed and gossiped for quite a while. Before long, things were back to normal, my tears only an uneasy memory.

By the time Grandpap returned with the truck filled with aunts and uncles and cousins, we had everything ready and I was my usual, happy self again. I had a new mission in life.

My grandma had faith in me, even if I didn't. I had decided I would be a writer, no matter how long it takes.

CHAPTER THIRTEEN
The Truth About Hobos

"Anthony, just look at this child!" Those were the first words out of Mum's mouth as I stepped off the train. Not "Hello," or "I've missed you!"

"Just look at her," she continued. "She's skin and bones!"

"What's wrong?" I demanded.

"Just look at ya. Were ya not happy there?"

"It was fine, Mum."

"But ya've lost more weight. Didn't ya eat?"

"Of course I did, but I guess I worked it all off in the fields. It might be getting cooler, but it's warm during the day, especially when you're picking vegetables and hauling them over to the trucks."

Mum looked a little doubtful, but Papa gave her a look and she let it go. "Don't worry about it, Margaret. She looks all right to me," and he gave me a big hug. "And how are you, young lady?"

"Fine," I told him. "It feels good to be home."

Mum finally hugged me, too, but I know she was still worried about my weight.

We said goodbye to Aunt Martha and Uncle Randall, who had come to pick up Denny, and left. I had so much to tell them that I chatted all the way home.

"And last night, Grandma made a cake for me. We celebrated my birthday a few days early. And she got me a book. I haven't read that much yet, but it's getting really good."

"What book is it?" Mum asked.

"*A Tale of Two Cities* by Charles Dickens."

"Oh. I've read that. It's a great book. I liked the part where you find out Madame Lafarge- wait. I'm not going to spoil it for you, but you're right. It's very good."

I enjoyed talking with my parents about books and the family and life on the farm. As we sat around the table that night, I brought all the news from the family and our adventures from the past few weeks. I also told them about the hilarious pranks Grandpap and Merle played on everyone. Papa was almost in hysterics when I told him about Merle and Denny and the donkey egg.

"Trust me," I said through his laughter, "we definitely had a good time there."

Mum looked dubiously at me. "Ok," she said as she went to refill her teacup. "I just hope Dale has enough ta eat. At least one of my children should be well fed."

"What do you hear from Dale?" I asked, ignoring her remark.

"Nothing," she said as she put away the sugar and slammed the cabinet door closed. "The last letter we got from him was the one that came two weeks before ya left."

I didn't ask any more questions because I could tell Dale was a sore spot with her again. Of course, it made me angry with him as well. After all, he wasn't the one who had to be home with Mum while she was so cross all the time.

After dinner, I wandered outside and sat down on the back porch. It was chilly, but it was also quiet. With so many aunts, uncles, and cousins, I hadn't had much quiet time at the farm, and I wanted to enjoy it. I watched as the clouds began moving in to bring rain, maybe even snow. I pulled my jacket closer around me in an attempt to keep warm, but it was no use, so I got up to go in. That's when I noticed there were several men standing in the area over between our fence and the railroad tracks. I figured they were bums who'd left their families. It made me think of Dale, and I didn't want anything to do with men like that, so I went inside, said good night to Mum and Papa, and went to my room. I fully intended to read my book, but I fell asleep about two minutes after I got into bed.

The next day was Saturday and Mum allowed me to sleep in. When I got up, I went to the kitchen to have morning tea with her. I just had to ask her about the factory. I had to know if I was supposed to go back to work, or if I'd be allowed to go back to school.

I approached the subject cautiously. "I know tomorrow's Sunday, so we'll be going to church, but what do you want me to do Monday?"

Mum looked confused. "What do ya mean? What are ya ta do fer yer birthday?"

I wasn't sure how she would react, so I asked a little more directly. "What should I do on Monday morning; get ready for work or get ready for school?"

"Oh," Mum said. After a short pause, she forced a smile and said, "Mr. Reed held yer job fer ya. Isn't that wonderful?"

Seriously? She thought it was wonderful?

"Sure," I said, forcing a fake smile in return.

There was a momentary silence, then Mum took my hands and spoke gently. "Honey, I know ya'd really rather go ta school, but right now, we need the money. I know the newspapers say that the economy is improving, but we can barely eat as it is. Especially with me being the only one working here. Ta make the rent and pay fer clothes, we still need yer money. It'll really help us ta have ya working. I hope ya understand."

I smiled, remembering Grandma's words, and my heart melted just a bit. "I understand, Mum. I really do. I do want to go to school, but it can wait."

"Are ya sure?" she asked, relief stealing over her features.

"Yes," I said. "I'm sure." And for once, I felt like I truly understood. Sometimes, things are just bigger than me. Sometimes I need to be patient.

Mum gave me a hug, and then went to get the freshly washed clothes. I sipped my tea and tried to accept the truth in silence. I wasn't a bit surprised that Mr. Reed had let me keep my job, because I had the funny feeling that he was paying me less than he was paying the other women in our area. At the same time, I'd so hoped that the job would be gone, and then perhaps I could've gone back to school.

Maybe it was just as well, I reasoned. I wasn't sure I would've been happy returning to school either. The last time I'd seen the kids from school was at the Fourth of July picnic, and that whole episode had left me with mistrust about who my real friends were. At least Anna would be at the factory, and somehow that made the thought of cleaning chickens more appealing than the idea of returning to school.

After breakfast, I offered to help take out the clothes to be dried. Mum and I gathered them and went outside to hang them on the lines.

"Hey, what's this?" I asked Mum. Beside our back porch, on the concrete, there was a chalk drawing. It wasn't a stick figure, or a drawing like a child would make, but rather a round, curvy drawing of a cat.

"I'm not sure," Mum shrugged, "but it appeared about a month ago. Even after the rain erased it, someone put it back again, and I thought it was sort of cute, so I just left it."

"Hmm," I said, wondering about it. We walked over and began folding the dry clothes currently hanging on the line.

Mum and I chatted for a few minutes. Then I noticed that there were several men standing near the gate, not too far from the train yards.

"What are those men doing?" I asked Mum.

Mum looked over at the men. "They don't seem ta be doing anythin'." Then she went right back to work.

"Maybe they should be," I said under my breath.

"What do ya mean by that?"

"Oh," I responded rather coldly, "I just think that maybe they should be out working."

I was thinking about that Hooverville we'd passed on the way to Grandpap's farm, and how I hadn't seen that many men there. I thought about how many men had jumped on the trains, leaving their wives and children behind. I thought about Mr. Fitzgerald, leaving his wife to live alone in her car, and I thought about Dale and how he abandoned us. These men weren't even out looking for work; they were just standing around talking.

"Well, they work when they can," Mum said, pulling down a sheet and folding it.

I grunted. "Then why are they wandering around here? They don't look like they're working to me."

Mum stopped and turned to look me in the eye. "Sometimes 'tis just not that simple, Beth. Now hush."

About the time we finished hanging the wet clothes, I heard a voice say, "Hello, Mrs. Sundo."

"Good morning, Charlie," Mum answered. "How did ya do?"

"I got some work at that store you were talking about. It only lasted two days, but it really helped. Thank you, ma'am."

"Yer welcome," Mum said cheerily, as she gathered the clothes baskets and headed into the house.

When we were inside, I asked "Who was that?"

"Oh, just a man I know. He's just a little down on his luck."

"What does that mean?"

"It means he's down on his luck," she reiterated.

"Why didn't Papa go get whatever job this Charlie guy was talking about?" I was indignant.

"Well," Mum began as she prepared to iron the clothes. "He just needed a little extra help is all."

I felt my face growing hot with anger as those beautiful words from Grandma became a distant memory. "You mean you and Papa told him where there was a job, but Papa didn't go get it, so I have to go back to work now?"

"Aye-yah, I guess that would about sum it up," she said shortly.

"But that's not fair!" I complained. "Why didn't Papa just go get that job so that I could go back to school?"

"Ya heard him," she said sharply, laying down the clothes. "The job only lasted a couple of days. Yer father could've had it, but he would've been back out of work within the week. I know ya don't really want ta work, but ya'll have ta fer now. Now, let me alone on the subject."

There were no more words spoken as we went back to folding clothes. Afterwards, I went up to my room to read. There was an uneasy silence the rest of the weekend, but the anger had subsided by Sunday night.

Monday wasn't exactly the happiest of birthdays since I had to go back to the factory, but at least I got to see Anna again.

"Good morning, Anna! I'm back!"

"Tis about time, too," she said, running up to hug me. "Ya aren't expectin' me ta be cleaning all these chickens by meself, are ya?"

"Hey, I got back as fast as I could."

She looked me up and down. "So, ye're back. When did ya turn 15?"

"Today."

"Well, now that's wonderful. Ya can stay here with me during the days. Oh! and I bought ya a present, but 'tis at home. I wasn't sure when ya were goin' ta be back."

We slid into our boots, and our friendship picked up right where it left off. I told her all about the farm life and funny moments, the work and my family. For a short few hours, I was glad to be back.

That was short-lived, of course. It didn't take long for Harold to come over and harass me, and I overheard Mrs. Fredericks gossiping about someone, and I avoided Mr. Reed at all costs. I did have fun talking with Anna all day, but I was still glad when the whistle blew that evening. I was more than ready to go home.

My birthday celebration was very quiet. We had dinner and vanilla cake with chocolate icing. After dinner, I was putting away my clean clothes when I noticed a small tear in the pocket of one of my dresses. It would take more than my poor sewing skills to fix, so I went downstairs to ask Mum for help.

"Mum, could you sew something for me?" I called, but there was no answer.

"Mum?" I descended the stairs and still didn't hear anything. "Papa?"

Then I heard the back door open and shut. "Mum?"

"Aye-yah?"

"Where were you?" I asked.

"Outside," she said simply, and before I could ask what she was doing, she asked, "What did ya need?"

"I just needed to know if you could help me. I have to sew a pocket on my dress." And I didn't even give Mum's trip outside another thought.

Until it happened again.

It was about three nights later. The birthday present Anna had given me was a pad of paper and a new pen because she knew I wanted to be a newspaper reporter. My goal was to practice writing in it a little bit each night about whatever was going on at the factory or in the neighborhood. I was working on it at my desk when I noticed Mum through the window. She was walking through the backyard carrying two cups of coffee and a small bag. She looked around into the darkness before she passed through the gate. From near the train yards I saw some men approaching her. I almost jumped when I saw them. They were big men dressed in old clothes. For a moment, I was scared. Then I realized who one of the men was.

It was Papa.

I watched as my parents passed out coffee and food, then they stood and talked with these men for several minutes.

They were feeding the homeless men that were stealing rides on the trains!

I thought about those Hoovervilles again, and I lost my temper.

I marched downstairs and sat down in one of the dining room chairs and waited. After several minutes, Mum came back in alone. Papa had left with the other men.

"What's going on?" I asked Mum, an accusing tone sharpening my voice. Startled, she jumped.

"Beth!" Her hand flew over her heart. "What're ya doing here?"

"I was watching you two," I said rather coldly. "What's going on out there?"

"What do ya mean?" Mum said, as she started putting away the clean dishes.

I stood up and stared at her. "Why are you and Papa out there helping those men?"

"I told ya, Beth, those men are down on their luck. They need some help."

I stood up. "Why do you and Papa need to be the ones to help? Don't you know who those men are? They're bums!"

Mum spun around and faced me straight on. "Elizabeth, I don't ever want ta hear ya say anything like that again. Ya don't know anything about these men."

"I know that they're the type of men who've left their families, just like Dale left us. I don't see how you can help someone who leaves their family like he left ours. You're giving them the food that we can barely afford ourselves!"

"Elizabeth!" Mum spoke sharply to me, but I continued.

"Every time I get my pay, I give you my money! I don't get to keep any of it. Then you turn around and give it to the men who are at the train yard? How can you do that? You know how much I hate working at that factory! How can you make me work, and then give them the money that I make?"

"Because," my mum shouted at me, "I'd hope that somewhere there's a family that's helping Dale!"

I stood, glaring at my mother. She glared back. The silence was terrifying. I don't remember ever being as mad at my family as I was at that moment. I felt I was being forced to work at the factory while Dale went out and did what he wanted and my parents gave away my earnings.

I felt there was nothing else to say, so I stormed upstairs.

It was almost a week before I could talk civilly to my parents. I know I was trying to learn to speak up for myself and not hold in the anger, but I felt the old me returning; the one that would get quiet whenever I was angry.

So for the next week, I was rude and sulky, and I knew it. But I couldn't help it. I felt betrayed!

Because the November air made the mornings colder, I had no trouble ignoring Mum on our way to work each day. The winds were so sharp that we had to bundle up and walk quickly in order to keep warm. But the evenings were not as easy because Mum and Papa were there at the dinner table. Then they'd go out to feed any men who were around and wanted to eat. I'd clean up the dishes and go up to my room as quickly as possible.

This went on for several days, and I was just getting back to being able to talk to them again when we received a letter from Dale. It read:

Dear Mum and Papa, I know I can't be there for Thanksgiving this year, but here is five dollars. I want you to take it and buy a turkey for Thanksgiving dinner. If you eat at exactly twelve o'clock, I will eat at that same time. Know that I will be thinking of you at that hour. Give Beth a hug for me. I love you,

Dale

Mum cried and cried as she read the letter. She went on and on about how sweet it was for him to make sure we had Thanksgiving dinner.

Seriously? He works, sends money, and gets all kinds of praise for "providing for us." I'd worked every day for the last six months to provide meals and shelter. I never even got a "thank you," but let Dale send us five dollars, and he's just short of a saint!

"I know what we should do," Mum continued. "Why don't we ask David, Ronnie, Jim and the others ta join us?"

"That would be a wonderful way to spend the money," Papa said.

"Maybe we could even get a roast beef instead?" Mum asked.

'That's not a bad idea," Papa said. 'We can make the money go further that way."

"I can't believe this horsefeathers," I muttered to myself. I threw down my napkin and stormed to my room, not caring to finish my lunch. They really wanted those men to be with us for Thanksgiving dinner? I spent the rest of the day in my room.

That night, Papa was gone during dinner, and Mum asked me to help her carry food out to the men. I almost exploded.

"You've got to be joking," I snapped. "You know how I feel about those men!"

"Fine," Mum said, looking totally defeated, "Ya don't have ta help me feed them, but could ya at least make the coffee fer me? They could use some before they go off ta wherever they're staying fer the night."

"All right," I agreed, just to get her out of the house. "I'll start a pot now."

Mum's eyes brightened. "Thank ya. It feels odd going out there without yer father beside me."

She stood and started gathering the bags of food and the coffee cups. "I'll get these out ta the men, and I'll send Jim ta the house fer the coffee."

"Great," I muttered. "I'll be here."

Two seconds later, Mum was out the door and I was pouring water into the percolator. I turned on the stove and let the water boil. I really hated that I was helping my parents in the very act I so detested.

Eventually, there was knock at the door.

"Wait a minute!" I called, because I didn't want any of those men in my house without my parents there for protection. The door burst open before I could get there. I ran over to shut it and found myself staring at a boy.

A boy my own age; perhaps younger.

"Yes?" I said.

He grinned sheepishly. "Hi. My name's Jim. Your mother said I should come up here to pick up the coffee."

"Uhm, sure," I said, still in shock. All this time, I assumed Jim was a grown man, but he was just like me. "Here, have a seat. It'll be ready in a minute. May I make you a cup of tea?"

"Thanks! It's really warm in here," he said, taking the chair closest to the door. "And it smells like a home."

I wasn't sure what to say, so I handed him a cup and asked where his home was.

"Virginia," he said.

I looked at him. "Virginia? What are you doing in Pennsylvania?" I asked, pulling up a chair.

His sheepish grin never faded. "I came up here looking for work. I figured, 'Hey, I'm old enough. Why shouldn't I help out my family?' so I packed up what I could and hopped a train up north, and here I am."

"How old are you?"

"Thirteen."

"Aren't you scared of being alone?" I asked him, pouring him some of the hot tea left over from dinner.

"Nah, not really. Most of the older guys look out for me, like Ronnie and Dave. They're great. They take home some food for their families, they let me share work with them when they can, and then I can send some money home to my parents."

"Really? That's nice of them." I thought about Dale. I'd been so angry with him for leaving that I'd never thought of what it was like for him to leave, or about what he was going through out on the road.

I didn't really know what else to say, but thankfully Jim could talk enough for both of us.

"Oh, they're great. They take care of each other, they watch out for the younger fellows like me, and they let me stay with them at night. That way I'm not in danger from crazy men. You know, the kind that don't mind hurting kids?"

I shuddered to think of what kind of men he could be referring to. "So how did you know you could trust these men?"

"Oh, you talk with people, and they teach you things. Things like looking for that cat sign outside."

"What? The cat sign?" I asked, totally confused for a moment, then I remembered. "Oh! Are you talking about that chalk drawing of the cat out by my back porch?"

He sipped his tea again. "Yes. Don't you know what that means?"

"No."

Jim laughed. "It's the signal to other men that the woman who lives here is helpful and gives food. In some places, it's hard to find anyone to help you. They call you a bum, or maybe something worse. It's especially hard on us kids. Most of us are thrown in jail for riding the trains. But then there are places where whole neighborhoods work together, and everyone shares everything. That's why I like it here. Your folks don't mind helping, and they don't judge me unfairly."

I can't explain it, but it was like my heart was melting as he talked. All that anger just began to fade away. All this time, I hadn't thought about what Dale was going through, or why Mum and Papa felt the need to help others. I hadn't even thought about these men or where they were staying. Jim told me the dangers of riding on trains and the dangers of just being out on his own.

We talked for quite a while, until Mum came back with Ronnie so they could get the coffee. As the men were leaving, I told Mum not to worry about the dishes; that I'd take care of them. She looked pleasantly surprised as she left.

I'd just finished cleaning the kitchen when she returned with the now-empty coffee pot. I certainly wouldn't admit I was wrong to be acting like such a brat, but I did give her a hug and offer to make some of my specialty apple pies for Thanksgiving dessert.

"Do you think two pies will be enough? I could also try a mince-meat pie, if you want."

She looked quizzically at me. "Won't that be a lot for just the three of us?"

"Well, I don't know who all else is coming. Just let me know how many men you are inviting, and I can bake enough for all of us."

She smiled at me, and I knew I was forgiven. Things were better for Mum and me after that.

CHAPTER FOURTEEN
Tiny, Wonderful Christmas

One week later, there was a light snow on the ground, and wreaths and bows were beginning to cover the doors of all the stores downtown. Candles and lights twinkled in the windows, and everyone seemed to be in a cheerier mood than I'd seen in a long while. Christmas was coming, and I hoped that perhaps Dale would come home. I'd grown to love helping Mum and Papa as they helped the migrant men, but on the other hand, it made me miss Dale even more.

Still, Christmas was coming, and I was in such a good mood. I really wanted Christmas to feel like it had when I was little. I wanted a tree, gifts for Mum and Papa, and I wanted to get something for Anna as well. I couldn't afford much, but I desperately wanted to get her something she could put in her hope chest. She was probably the closest friend I'd ever had.

But most of all, I wanted to surprise Mum and Papa with a ham. It's not my favorite dish, but Mum loves it. I was determined to find enough money to pay for it. For weeks, I grabbed every spare penny in the house and hid it in a small coin purse

I had hidden in my room. If I had change left over from a trip to the store, I took two cents of it and put it in there. If I found money on the street, straight into the purse it went.

One Saturday, I told Mum I wanted to spend the day at Aunt Martha's store so I could see if there were any Christmas presents I wanted to buy. That was partially true, but I'd also asked Aunt Martha if she could help me sew an apron for Mum.

I left early that Saturday morning and arrived just as she was opening up for business.

"Good mornin' to ya, Beth," she said as I walked up the porch steps. "How are ya?"

"Good, thanks. Where is everyone?"

"Well, I'm sorry ta say, but yer Uncle Randall took Dennis with him to deliver some packages ta a store in Everton," she said as she gathered her orders for the day. "I'm on me own today, so I will only be able ta help ye between customers."

"That's fine," I told her. "If I don't get finished today, I can work on it again next Saturday."

"All right. I have to go in back for a moment, but why don't ya look around at the material ta see if there is something that strikes yer fancy?"

"All right," I said with a grin. "Thank you."

"All these materials are regular priced, but I can still give ya a good discount on them. And those near the back of the store are even cheaper because I just need ta get rid of them. Look around and see what ya might want."

Her home was in the back of the store, so she disappeared into the kitchen while I looked around. There were some nice tea towels that would be great for Anna, but I wasn't sure I could afford them. I thought it best to wait before deciding on her gift. Looking around some more, I found that there wasn't really anything that I wanted for Papa. I thumbed through some books, looked at some suspenders, then browsed some hats, but no luck.

Someone was knocking at the back door, and I thought it was a little strange. The store was open, so why not come through the front? I started to go back there to open it and realized Aunt Martha had already answered it.

"Good day," she said to the two men standing on her back porch.

"Hello, Mrs. Avens. Do you have anything for us?"

She smiled. "Aye-yah. Just hold on a minute." She turned and went to the counter and pulled out a coat. Then, as an afterthought, she grabbed a bag of cookies. "Here's the coat, and here are some cookies fer yer son, Mr. Haggard."

A large smile covered the man's face. "Thank you, Mrs. Avens," he said. "Bobby will love the cookies. We haven't been able to afford sugar or sweets at our house in a long time. Thank you."

"'Tis no trouble," she said. "And we had the extra coat as well. I hope ya get the job."

"Thank you, ma'am," he said, and they both left.

Aunt Martha didn't know I could see her, and she continued about her business as if nothing had happened. The sick feeling I had the first day at the factory returned. For the first time, I wasn't angry for myself. I was angry that things were so rough for these poor men who wanted to work, were willing to work, but couldn't find work.

It was cruel.

Then I thought of Papa. What present could I possibly get that wouldn't remind him that I had a job and he didn't? I looked out of the window and onto the snowy ground, and I thought of the perfect gift. I'd seen some of the men's sweaters, and I thought of one that would keep him warm whenever he was out looking for a job.

I hurried back to the shelves and looked through the sweaters again. I found one that was thick and black, and I thought it would also be the perfect size for him.

Taking it to the counter, I held it up for Aunt Martha to see as she walked back into the room. "What do you think of this sweater?"

"That looks fabulous," she told me. "And since 'tis a close-out item, I can get it fer ya whole-sale."

"What does that mean?"

"It means I can knock another twenty-three cents off that price."

"Really?" I screamed without meaning to. "That's wonderful! Now I need to find some material for Mum's apron."

I looked through the more expensive materials near the front, and I saw some that were nice, but they weren't what I really wanted. Then I searched the reduced priced materials in the back, and that's where I found it. It was green with little red apples on it. The green and red were perfect for Christmas, but it could be worn all year 'round.

"Tis a nice pattern, Beth," Aunt Martha said when I brought it to her. "And this is on a close-out, so ya can have it fer free."

"Free?" I practically screamed.

"Yes, 'tisn't enough for a full dress, so I was going ta give it away anyway. Make it my Christmas present ta ya."

"Thank you!" I said with a huge hug.

Grabbing some paper and a pencil, I started figuring out how much money I had. With all I had saved up, and after paying for Papa's sweater, I could buy those tea towels for Anna and still have almost enough for the ham.

Entering the back room for some privacy, I turned my attention back to the material, turning it this way and that, trying to figure out which way the print would look best for the apron I wanted to make. I wasn't sure where to start, so I got another piece of paper and drew a picture of how I wanted it to look. I had no doubt Aunt Martha would know exactly how to cut it.

Just as I finished, she came into the back room.

"Look! I drew a picture so you could see what it looks like!"

"Hmm," she said in a hesitant tone.

I was crushed. "What's wrong with it?"

"Tis nice, but ya've told me yerself that ya don't have the patience ta do somethin' as intricate as this. Are ya sure ya want ta make it this way?"

I eyed the picture. It was a full-length apron; the top went around the neck and the main segment covered the entire front of the dress.

"What's wrong with it?" I questioned again.

"Nothin' is wrong," she said, eyeing the picture, "but look at the details. Ya'd have ta make it in two parts, the upper bodice and the lower apron. That's goin' ta mean a lot of time. I just want ta make sure that's what ya want ta do."

I looked at the picture I had created and then at the beautiful materials in front of me.

"Yes," I said adamantly. "I'm willing to do this. Won't Mum be proud?"

"She certainly will be," she said. "Not ta mention shocked."

"Why? Because I—Aw! Aunt Martha!" I shrieked, and she started laughing.

For the rest of the morning, any time there wasn't a customer, we were cutting patterns and pinning parts together. After that, we went to work on her sewing machine. She showed me how to place the materials and sew them together. I had to go really slowly on the machine, because I wanted to be able to say I had done the whole thing myself. Soon, most of the apron was finished.

"Ya'll have ta put the lace trim on yerself, or ya'll need ta come back on another Saturday," she said when we were almost finished. "What do ya think?"

"I love using the sewing machine, but I don't know if I can get over here again before Christmas."

"Well, that sort of lace should really be done by hand and not on the machine. I could sew the trim on fer ya," she offered.

"Um, that's nice," I stammered, "but- but I want to be able to say that I finished it on my own." I looked her in the eyes, half scared and half hoping she wouldn't be mad. "Is that all right?"

She smiled. "I understand."

"Do you think I can finish it?" I asked.

"Sure," she said, grabbing a box of straight pins. "But you'll need some patience. Let me help ya pin this tagether. And ya'll probably want ta hide it. I have a bag ya can use, and then she can't see what ya have in it."

"That's a great idea," I said. We spent the next two hours pinning the trim to the edges and practicing the stitches I would need to make the lace stay on properly. When we finished, I hid my sewing in a bag with the other presents so that I could head home.

"Thank you, Aunt Martha," I said as I headed to the door. "I appreciate your help."

"'Tis no problem. Button up yer coat and keep warm on the way home."

"Yes, ma'am," I said, stepping out onto the front porch. I looked around for a minute and stepped back inside. "You know," I told her, "there's a little snow on the ground, but it isn't really cold out here."

Aunt Martha joined me on the porch. "Yer right. 'Tis warm out here. Maybe the snow will melt early."

"Maybe," I said. "I'll let you know how the apron turns out."

"Good. I'll be seein' ya on Christmas Day."

"Oh, good," I said. I thanked her again and left for home.

As soon as I walked through the door, I ran to my room to hide my treasures. Even though there wouldn't be enough money left over for pretty ribbons and bows, it would be worth it when Mum and Papa saw the ham and the presents.

Pulling the gifts out of the bag, I felt like a miser looking over vast riches. I calculated over and over how I could get the last of the money for the meat, and maybe add enough for ingredients for a pie. I thought that would be the best way to let Aunt Martha know how much I appreciated her help. Finally, I had to hide the gifts in my room and go downstairs to do my Saturday chores.

Every night that week I worked quietly in my room. By the next Friday, I had completed the apron and ironed it. Saturday was spent wrapping presents with any bright colored paper I could find and then going on a search for cola bottles. Glass cola bottles can be sold back to the store for a nickel apiece, and I found three. That, added to the money I already had, was enough for me to take a trip to the butcher shop and order the ham.

Lastly, I asked Mum if we had enough for me to bake one apple pie especially for Aunt Martha.

"Sure," she said. "I think it would be best if it were warm and fresh. Perhaps ya should get up early and bake it on Christmas morning."

I knew that idea wouldn't work, because I'd already made arrangements with the butcher shop for that morning. I couldn't figure out how on earth I could get to Mr. Heckle's shop and bake the pie all in the same morning.

By the week of Christmas, I'd decided to get the pie started as soon as we got home from the Christmas Eve service at church. I peeled and cut the apples, gathered all the sugar and spices, and prepared the crust. Once I put it into the oven, I ran to make sure all my gifts were wrapped as perfectly as possible and returned just in time to remove the pie and let it cool in the pantry.

I'd planned and planned for the next day. I just knew I'd die if they found out about my big surprise before I could pull it off, so I wound up my alarm clock and set if for early the next morning. When the alarm went off, I got up, got dressed, and ran as fast as I could down the streets of Allan. I came around the corner just in time to see Charlie Heckle open the door to his shop.

"Good morning, Mr. Heckle," I said.

"Good morning, Elizabeth," he said with a chuckle. "You weren't kidding me when you said you wanted to get here early."

"I want to get it into the oven before Mum wakes up," I told him. "Is it ready?"

"Yes, it is. Do you have the money?"

I felt the pride swelling in my chest as I handed him the coin purse full of money. "I do."

Mr. Heckle counted the change. "Beth, you did very well with your money. I'm impressed that you saved up enough for a family dinner. I must admit, there aren't many girls your age who would think of their families before themselves."

My cheeks warmed at the compliment. I didn't say anything, except, "Thank you."

Mr. Heckle pulled the precious prize from the refrigerated area of the store, and I gazed intently at it as he wrapped and tied it with a string. It was small, and it probably wouldn't go far, but I was proud of it.

I grabbed the package, went to Anna's house to drop off her present, then headed straight home. When I snuck into the house, I found biscuits sitting on top of the stove. I knew Mum must be up, but she was nowhere to be found.

I didn't even bother to remove my coat as I got everything ready. I took the first pan I could find and positioned the ham in the middle of it. Then I put the pan on the middle of the table and left the kitchen.

"Beth?" I heard Mum call from upstairs.

"I'm here, Mum!" I called, trying to sound nonchalant as I took off my jacket.

"Goodness, Beth!" she scolded as she and Papa headed downstairs. "Where on earth have ya been? Yer aunt and uncle are going ta be here any minute, and I need help making the lunch!"

"I'm sorry. I had to take Anna her Christmas present."

I stood quietly and smiled as Mum and Papa descended the stairs. She wasn't really angry, I could tell, but she continued to fuss at me as we went back into the kitchen. I sat down at the table and began to giggle because both she and Papa passed right by the ham platter about four times.

Mum kept fussing, Papa was brewing morning coffee, and neither one of the realized it was sitting there.

Then I heard, "I also think I need ya ta run down ta the butcher shop, and…"

Papa turned to see why Mum stopped in mid-sentence, then followed her gaze to the middle of the table.

After several seconds, Mum finally spoke. "Oh, Anthony, 'tis beautiful."

"Yes, it is," he replied.

"Oh, Anthony, ya shouldn't have!"

"Wait, I didn't…" Then it seemed to dawn on both of them.

"Do you like it?" I squealed.

"You? You bought it?" Papa asked.

I beamed. "Yes, sir."

"Oh, Beth, 'tis wonderful," Mum exclaimed, wiping away happy tears as she came to give me a hug. "I am so blessed. First me son buys us a Thanksgiving dinner, and now me daughter's given us a Christmas feast. I'm so proud of our children!" She wiped at her eyes again.

I'd hoped it didn't remind Papa that he didn't have a job, but I didn't have anything to worry about. He simply walked over and hugged Mum and me.

"I'm proud of you, Beth," he said. "How on earth did you manage to do that?"

"Just a little at a time," I told him.

"I should get started baking," Mum said as she went to the sink to wash her hands. Immediately, we heard a knock at the front door. Papa went to answer it and returned a few minutes later with Aunt Martha's family behind him.

"Martha!" Mum screamed, "Come look at the wonderful present me daughter brought us!"

"What?" Aunt Martha said, obviously looking around for the apron.

"Yer staring at it," Mum replied.

"Oh, Heaven's above!" Aunt Martha said. "The ham? Elizabeth bought the Christmas dinner?" She stared at me, and I couldn't help the feeling of pride that overcame me.

"Well, jiminy!" Uncle Randall said, "Isn't that something! I can't wait for my son to be old enough to buy me dinner."

Everyone laughed. As the adults went on and on about what I'd done, I helped prepare the potatoes and then went to the living room to wait for lunch. I looked around at the presents, wishing I could have bought a tree, but was content with the gift I had already given them. I didn't think anyone even noticed the lack of a tree, as happy as they already were. Perhaps next year I could get one. Grabbing my newest book, I curled up in a chair to read. I had barely started when Dennis came bounding into the room.

"My mum says we're having ham for dinner instead of chicken," he chirped happily. "I think that's grand. Mum said I should tell you 'thank you.' She says you bought it with your own money. If I had money, I wouldn't buy food. I'd probably buy more toy soldiers. Did you really buy it just for all of us? Thank you for dinner. Do you know what we got you for Christmas?"

I laughed. "You're welcome," I told him. "What did you get me for Christmas?"

"I can't tell you," he said, "but I know you'll like it. We have one at home, and I know you like ours."

"Oh, are you sure?" I asked, trying to get some information out of him. "And how do you know that I like that one?"

"Because I saw you looking at it, and I know you were listening. Did I show you my new toys?"

Dennis wasn't making any sense, and he could never stay on one topic for very long. I had no idea what the gift could be, so I sat in the living room floor and played with Dennis and his new toys for a while.

I was starving by the time Aunt Martha called us to lunch. I hadn't thought to eat breakfast, and Mum was so happy about the ham that she hadn't thought to fuss at me about not eating.

"Finally," Uncle Randall said as we headed into the dining room. "I'm famished."

I looked at the lovely dining table. It was probably the best Christmas dinner we'd had since the stock market crashed. There were sweet potatoes, biscuits, corn, and asparagus.

"Oh, Mum, it's beautiful!" I said as we sat down to say grace.

Everyone loved the ham. Mum had done a beautiful job with it, and everyone went on and on about how wonderful the food was. It was so grand, and everyone was having so much fun talking and laughing that I forgot about even opening the presents.

But Dennis didn't. "Can we open the presents now?" he started whining as we finished dinner.

"In a minute, Dennis," Aunt Martha scolded. "Maybe everyone wants their dessert before we go in there."

"Oh, let the boy go get the presents," Papa laughed. "We can all go, and we can have dessert afterwards."

I noticed Aunt Martha and Uncle Randall exchange a funny look, but I couldn't figure out what it meant.

"Come on," Mum chirped. "I think it would be lovely ta have our pies after we open presents."

We all rose from our chairs and went towards the living room, but Aunt Martha and Uncle Randall still were hesitant. Within only a few moments, all the presents were opened, and everyone was chatting wildly. Papa was modeling the new sweater I had bought him, and Mum was admiring a journal book that Aunt Martha had given her. I received a new pad of writing paper and a new book to read.

"Here, Mum," I said, handing her the present I made.

"What's this?"

"It's your present, silly."

"But, Beth, ya've given me so much already. Ya bought me something else as well?"

"No, Mum," I said, smiling at Aunt Martha. "I made it."

Mum cocked an eyebrow. "Really? I wonder what it could be."

Her fingers gently removed the paper and pulled it away. She pulled out the apron and held it up to get a better look at it. It was so pretty, even I had trouble believing I'd made it.

After a moment of silence, I asked, "Mum? Don't you like it?"

Her eyes filled with tears once more, and she smiled. "Ya made this?"

"Yes," I told her.

"I can't believe ya made this. 'Tis so beautiful. Ya did such fine work."

"Aunt Martha helped me cut it," I admitted.

"But she did all the sewing," Aunt Martha added.

"Elizabeth, 'tis lovely. It's just that, I know ya hate ta sew, and ya go and give me such a beautiful gift. Ya bought that beautiful ham along with the perfect gift fer yer father. It's just that..."

"It's just that we're so proud of you," Papa said. "You aren't a little girl anymore. You're such a young lady now."

I thought they were both going to cry, but fortunately there was a knock at the door.

"Who on earth could that be?" Mum asked, slipping on her new apron.

Uncle Randall jumped up and answered the door. "Oh, good!" he shouted. "It's here!" He moved out of the way and a young man entered the house.

I jumped up, hoping it was Dale.

But it wasn't.

"Here you go, Mr. Avens," the young man said. "I'm sorry I was late. We forgot to get the key to the truck. I had to go back to my house."

"That's okay," he said as he went out the door.

"Where is he going?" Mum asked.

"He's going ta get yer present from the back of the truck," Aunt Martha said, jumping up to follow him. "Put it in here, gentlemen!"

Before I knew it, the man was helping Uncle Randall place a radio in our living room. A radio!

"Oh, my!" Mum screamed.

"Randall, my good man," Papa declared, "This is such a nice gift. It's too much!"

"'Tisn't as expensive as it looks," Aunt Martha told him.

"I've seen those at yer store," Mum said. "I know how much they cost!"

"Aye-yah, but I got this one at a special sale, and I didn't have ta pay that much. I promise."

Mum looked doubtful, but then she thanked Aunt Martha profusely.

"This would be prefect, especially when we want ta know the news."

"Aye-yah, indeed," Aunt Martha told her, "and have ya heard one of President Roosevelt's Fireside Chats? 'Tis so nice ta be able ta hear the president's voice talkin' directly ta ya."

"It's wonderful," Papa said. "Now where shall we put it?"

"It needs to be by a plug," Uncle Randall said.

Mum and Papa looked at each other. "Do we have any electric outlets, Anthony?"

"Of course, we do," Papa said. Everyone looked around.

"Where?" I asked.

"On the light socket in the dining room."

We followed him into the dining room and looked up at the light.

"Hmm," Mum mused. "Is that the only one?"

We spent the next twenty minutes looking around downstairs for another electric outlet, but the only ones in our house were all in the light fixtures.

"Well, you know what that means?" Papa said. "We'll just have to clean off the table and put it on top."

"Oh, no ya don't, Anthony Sundo!" Mum responded. "You'll not be doin' such a thing on me nice table!"

"Don't be silly, Margaret," he told her. "We can put a blanket on the table first. I promise not to scratch it. And eventually, I'll make a stand for it."

"All right," she agreed, "but I'd better not see even one scratch."

"I have a great idea," Aunt Martha said. "Why don't we eat our pie while listenin' ta the radio?"

"That's a grand notion!" Mum said, then she looked over at me.

"Aunt Martha, I have something to give to you and Uncle Randall," I told her.

"What is it, me dear?"

"I'll show you," I told her. She followed me into the kitchen, and I took out the fresh apple pie. "I baked this for you, to say thank you for helping me with the apron."

"Oh, 'tis lovely," Aunt Martha said, clapping her hands. Then she got real serious. "Ya know, I'm so proud of ya. I know yer parents are as well, but I don't think yer Mum could tell ya without cryin'. But look at ya. Ya didn't want ta go ta work, and here ya've paid fer a ham, provided a good Christmas fer yer parents, and learned ta bake and sew as well. I couldn't be any more proud of ya if ya were me own daughter."

"Thank you." I couldn't think of anything else to say, but she took care of that.

"Now, why don't we cut this pie and get it inta the dinin' room?" she said.

"Sounds good to me." And we started cutting.

By the time we returned to the dining room, everyone else had cleared the dishes and put the blanket and radio on one end of the table. We gathered around and stared intently as Uncle Randall turned it on and selected the frequency. After only a few moments, we were eating pie and hearing a man's voice reading "The Gift of the Magi" by O. Henry.

"This is so wonderful," I told Aunt Martha. "Mum, are we going to leave it there so that we can listen to it every night?"

"Well, I suppose so," Mum chuckled. "It might be a little in the way, but at least we have a radio now."

Best. Christmas. Ever.

CHAPTER FIFTEEN
Uncle Elton's Visit

Worst. January and February. Ever.

January was the most boring January in the history of the world. There was nothing going on, and I mean *nothing*. It was dark and cold in the mornings when we left for work, it was dark and cold in the evenings when we came home. There was always a light snow on the ground, but not enough for even a decent snowball fight. Not that I ever got to see my friends for a snowball fight.

Except on Sundays.

On Sundays, we went to church, and I saw a few girls from my school, but they would talk about stuff at school, and after a while, I began to feel left out.

And it wasn't just that I was left out of knowing what was happening at school, but it made me so sad to hear how well the new girls' basketball team was doing and know I wasn't part of it. Or how funny the new teacher was and knowing I'd never be able to be in his class.

We had nothing in common anymore, and it hurt. Eventually, I found myself talking with the other ladies of the church. Most of them had to work, too, and I felt I could relate to them.

That was also the month Uncle Elton sent us his letter. Since it was from Virginia, I thought it would be from Dale.

"No," Papa muttered, thinking aloud. "He's in Texas."

"He could've moved again."

"No," Mum cut in. "'Tis from me Uncle Elton."

"Well that's a nice surprise," Papa said. "What's the old man say?"

Mum was still reading, but she'd start muttering things like, "Oh, no," and "Oh, my!" Tears began to fill her eyes. She turned toward Papa.

"Anthony, it says here that there's been an accident! A coal mining accident. Two men were killed, and one is in a wheelchair."

"Oh, how awful!" I said.

Then she couldn't control her tears any longer. "And Anthony, Elton was hurt. 'Tis his arm. His right arm was crushed and is totally useless ta him now. He says he has no alternative but ta go ta the local asylum! And Anthony, he wants ta know if he could come ta stay with us for a week before he goes, because he may never get another chance ta visit."

"Of course he can, Margaret," Papa said, wrapping her in his strong arms. "I don't understand why you even have to ask. You know I admire your uncle. I can't even bear the thought of him having to live his life in an asylum. That's just plain ridiculous. Perhaps we can even find him a job here."

"With only one good arm?" Mum sobbed. "He's not a young man, and with only one good arm, he won't be able ta do any sort of physical labor."

"I know, but we'll have to start looking."

Uncle Elton was pretty much our only topic of conversation that night. We wracked our brains trying to think of work he could do. The next morning, Mum wrote to him to let him know he could definitely come for a visit. We set to cleaning Dale's room and airing out the bed. We didn't know when he might arrive, Mum said, so we had to be prepared.

I cleaned Dale's blanket and sheets, and I scrubbed the floor with hot, soapy water. In some ways, I was happy to help out, but I sort of felt like we were kicking Dale out of our lives. On the other hand, I suppose, I know if Dale were here, he would've offered to give up his bedroom anyway. Then he would have slept in the small room in the basement. That thought made the idea a little easier to deal with.

Two weeks later, Mum and I came home from work and found Uncle Elton sitting with Papa at the table, drinking tea. Mum was so excited as he got up from the table to hug her. His smile was as warm and friendly as I remember, and he was a strong looking man, yet a limp, withered arm hung loosely at his right side.

He hugged her with a strong left arm, and said, "Margaret, how are ya doin'?" I noticed that he still had a slight Irish accent, just like Mum.

"I'm fine," she said. "Tis ya I'm worried about. How are ya feeling? How long can ya stay with us?"

Uncle Elton lowered his eyes. "I can stay only two weeks. The asylum can take me at that time, and I don't know how long they'll hold the spot open." Then he reached over and gave me a big hug with his left arm. I saw the smile in his face, but there was a tear in his eye.

"How's my wee girl?" he asked. "I see she's not so wee in size nor in spirit, is she?"

"No, sir." I grinned.

"Well, I'd best be getting supper," Mum said. "I bet yer hungry."

"I'll take care of getting supper," I told her. "You sit down and visit."

Mum smiled. "All right, but I thought we might be making Hoover Stew. Everything is ready in the ice box. Do ya think ya can handle that?"

"Yes," I told her. "I've made it with you enough times. I can't mess it up."

After all, Hoover Stew, like the people in the Hoovervilles would eat, was basically spaghetti with hot dogs, peas, and carrots. Besides, I knew that if I was cooking, I wouldn't be told to leave. I got to stay in the kitchen and listen to the stories Uncle Elton told. He told us about the accident he was in, and how the men had been rescued, and the sad story of how two of them couldn't be saved. He told us about life in Virginia and then he reminisced about life in Ireland before he came to America with Mum and my grandparents. I enjoyed listening to them talk, and knowing I was being treated as an adult. I listened while I cooked and boiled the rich sauce.

After dinner, the grown folks did the dishes together while I got to sit and relax. I was watching Uncle Elton, and I realized that for the most part, you wouldn't really notice his arm after talking with him for a while.

Papa suggested we have tea in the living room, so we all went in and sat down. After Mum poured the tea, she sat down next to Papa, and he gently took her hand.

"Elton," Papa began, looking solemn, "Margaret and I have been talking. We want you to stay with us. We have some room, with Dale being gone and all. And with Margaret and Beth working, we think we can afford for you to stay here. I usually find some odd jobs to do, so you can help us out on days that I have work. What do you say?"

Uncle Elton sat for the longest time, staring into his cup of tea. He looked up, and gave a very firm, "I appreciate it, but no."

"But why?" I asked, and then I remembered I was only fifteen, and I was still expected to keep quiet in matters of adults.

Uncle Elton didn't seem to mind my question. "I can't stay here if I don't feel that I can help out in some way. I need ta have a job. At least at the asylum, I can work with some of the inmates. I can do something ta help earn my keep.

"Now, if ya don't mind," he said, standing, "I've had a long trip. I'm going on ta bed. Thank ya fer dinner."

He left so quickly that Mum had to bustle upstairs after him to settle him in. Papa and I continued to sit in the living room thinking. After a while, Mum came back downstairs to finish her tea. I asked her about the asylum he would be going to.

"What will it be like?" I asked.

Tears began to run down her cheeks. "Tis an awful place, I'm sure. That's where they keep criminals and insane people. I just know that it'll be terrible."

"So why does he have to go there?"

"Because, he has nowhere else to go," Papa said. "He lost his family several years ago during an influenza epidemic, so we're the only family he has left. There are no good places for him to go, and there are no jobs for a man with only one good arm."

I had what I thought was a brainstorm. "Why doesn't he go to Grandpap's farm?"

Mum took her handkerchief and wiped her eyes. "Me mum and da have asked him ta stay with them last week, but he refuses ta go. He won't even go see them, and my father is his own brother. Ya'd think he wouldn't feel like a burden ta his own brother."

Personally, I don't see why he would feel like a burden to anyone in his own family. Family is family, and family has to stick together and help each other out. But what do I know? Dale left. He said he did it to help out our family. Maybe it's some weird code grown-ups live by. Why wouldn't you help out family when you could?

Through the next two weeks, we had a lot of company. Since he wouldn't go see them, Grandma and Grandpap came to visit Elton. Everyone knew it was probably for the last time. They stayed with us almost a week. They tried talking to Elton, too, but with no luck. He'd have none of it and was determined to go to the asylum. There were a lot of tears when they left.

The day before he was supposed to leave, I went to Aunt Martha's store to buy some paper and pencils for Uncle Elton, so he could write to us. He had been right-handed, and I knew he'd have to learn to write all over again with his left. I thought paper and pencil for him to practice on might help, but I really just wanted to get out of the house. I was trying to think of something that would make him want to stay with us. He was strong and funny and so full of life. How could he want to be in an asylum surrounded by people who were either criminals or insane? And how could I convince him that he was hurting Mum and Papa?

I was trying so hard to come up with a solution when something fluttered in the corner of my eye. Turning, I saw a man in the window of the bank building. Then I realized what he was doing.

He was putting a 'Help Wanted' sign in the window! I took off running.

"What kind of job do you have?" I almost yelled as I ran into the front door of the bank.

"Whoa, whoa, young lady," the man in the office laughed. "I'm sorry, but it's not a job for little girl like you."

I wasn't sure if I liked what he was saying or not, but I continued with, "It's not for me. I'm checking for my uncle. Besides, I already have a job."

That seemed to impress him for some reason. "Oh. Well, we're looking for a man who can work nights as a security guard, to keep an eye on things and keep the furnace lit. Already had to fix the pipes once when they froze over and ruptured. Flooded half the building. I can't afford to let that happen again."

"My uncle could do that," I said. "He's lost his wife, so he doesn't have to be home at nights. He sometimes works on the furnace at our house." Okay, I sort of stretched the truth a little, but I know he used to have his own home and he mentioned working on his furnace that at some point, so I figured a little white lie wouldn't hurt.

"Sounds great," he said. "Can you go home and get him?"

I wasn't sure what to say. "There is just one problem," I said quietly.

He eyed me suspiciously.

"When you first see him, you may think he can't do the job. He was injured in a coal mining accident. His arm is hurt, but he's still strong. He's a good man, and I know he can do it if you'll just give him a chance."

He looked thoughtful for a minute. "His arm's hurt, you say?"

I nodded.

"But you think he could do this?"

I nodded again. "I know he can!"

"I'll tell you what, young lady, I need someone I can trust. You go home and get him, and I'll take down the sign. Bring him back here in fifteen minutes, and I promise not to look at anyone else until you get back."

"Yes, sir!" I yelled, not meaning to. "I'll hurry!"

I heard the man laughing as I ran out the door. I ran all the way home and slammed the door open. "Uncle Elton!" I hollered.

"Beth!" Mum said as I came flying through the door. "Don't be screaming. Yer uncle's upstairs. What's wrong?"

"Nothing," I said excitedly as I kept running up the stairs. "Uncle Elton!" I called, beating on the bedroom door. He opened the door, and I could see that he was in the middle of gathering toiletries to put back in his suitcase.

"What is it?"

"Uncle Elton, come with me!" I grabbed his good hand and practically pulled him down the stairs and through the door. "I have to show you something. I'll tell you about it on the way. Hurry!" He barely had time to grab his coat.

A few minutes later, we were entering the bank. Uncle Elton was desperately trying to fix his hair with his good hand. I had been in such a rush to get him to the bank that I hadn't noticed that he should've changed clothes and combed his hair.

"Here's my uncle," I gasped out, trying to catch my breath.

The man ignored the withered arm and reached out his left hand to shake hands with Uncle Elton. It was a small gesture, but it was kind. Uncle Elton appeared a little more relaxed as he shook hands with his left arm.

"How do you do, sir. I am Mr. Matlack. Won't you come into my office?"

Uncle Elton followed him into the office, and I waited in the lobby. After ten minutes, he came back outside. "Well?" I asked.

"Well, it seems I have a job."

I threw my arms around him and screamed for joy.

"It's not as good as it sounds," he said. "I've one week ta prove I can do the work. I can handle most of it, but I have ta go down ta the basement and stoke the fires each night. That's the only part of the job I'm not sure that I can handle."

"But you can do it, Uncle Elton!" I cried. "We can help. We can do it somehow."

"Well," he said, and I noticed that his hand was shaking. "We'll find out. Let's go talk ta yer mum and papa. I've an idea that may work."

Mum and Papa were thrilled to hear about the job, but they had the same concern Uncle Elton had. "How are you going to stoke those fires?" Papa asked.

"Well, I have an idea, if the offer ta stay here is still open."

"Of course it is," both of my parents said at the same time. Then Papa asked, "So what's the idea?"

"Well, Anthony, I insist on paying me way, ya know that. And I can do this, if yer willing ta help me. What if, on days ya don't have ta work, mind ya; what if ya came down ta the bank, just long enough ta help me stoke the fires?"

Papa's smile was immediate. "Elton, I'd love to help you."

"And," Uncle Elton continued, "I know that'd be hard on ya, but 'tis only really necessary on the cold, winter nights. As spring comes and the weather gets better, ya'll be getting more work, and I won't need as much help when 'tis warm."

"Uncle Elton, does this mean yer staying?" Mum asked excitedly.

"Only if ya'll help me and let me pay rent," he said.

Mum was so excited, she jumped up to hug him, and this time she wasn't crying. Then she took off to the kitchen and started preparing his lunch for him to take to work on his first night. I could tell that she was really thrilled. She always cooked when she was happy, and she made a lunch for him that was so big that I didn't think he could eat it all.

Yep, other than that, January was pretty boring. But it was still better than February.

CHAPTER SIXTEEN

Cold Snap

"I've got it! I've got it!"

"Got what?" I asked as Anna came screeching into the vat area one Monday morning.

"I've got some proof!" She pulled two sheets of paper from her apron pocket. "Look!"

I looked over the papers but couldn't make out what she was showing me. "These are just the sign-in sheets for our weekly pay."

"Right!" she said. "You know how we have ta sign our names when we get our pay?"

"Yes," I said, drying my hands and getting very interested.

"Look at these names. Here's mine, an' yers…"

"And here's Mum's, and Mrs. Johansson's."

"Exactly," she said. "Now, look at this paper I'm holdin.' 'Tis a list of each person in Reed's area, an' how much each person is ta be paid."

"So?"

"Well, I got this from bookkapein'. They make a list o' workers an' how much Reed should be givin' each person. That way, they're knowin' exactly how much ta give Reed so that he'll have enough money ta be payin' us."

"I think I understand," I murmured.

A sly smile crossed her face. "Look at this. Do ya recognize the name here, at the bottom o' this list?"

"Oh, my word!" I gasped. "I sure do!"

"Well, I don't!" She snatched the paper away from me and stared intently at it. "Nerts ta that. An' here I was, thinkin' I'd gone an' caught the rat in the act."

"Wait just a minute," I said. "I'm confused. Start at the beginning."

"Aye-yah," she said in a very depressed tone. "On the days we're ta be paid, the bookkapeer gives Reed two things. He gets a bag o' money an' a list o' how much he should be payin' each person. If any money's left over, he has ta be givin' it back ta the bookkaepers."

"And?" I asked, beginning to get impatient.

"Accordin' ta this, there's a lady named Mary Fitzgerald workin' in our area. But ta be sure, I don't know her. I thought Reed was makin' up a pretend person so he could kape her pay for his own self."

"Oh, he's keeping her money all right," I said angrily.

She stared at me in confusion. "Huh?"

"I told you I knew Mary Fitzgerald—and I do—but not because she works here. I know her because she used to live near us. Now she lives in her car."

"Then how did greedy auld Reed get her name?"

I thought about that for a minute. "Oh! I remember! I saw her here a couple of times on job interview days."

"So," she deduced aloud, "she was tryin' ta get a job here, and Reed wrote down her name, and then made it look like she was workin' here, so he could be kapein' her paycheck?"

"That would have to be how it happened," I guessed.

We sat down on a bench, temporarily forgetting our work, and tried to reconstruct Mr. Reed's plan. Could we be onto the truth, or were we just two kids with overactive imaginations?

"I just realized something," I said aloud.

"Aye-yah?"

"How did you know Mrs. Fitzgerald's name was the one faked if you didn't even know her?"

"Oh, tis here. Look back on the first paper I gave ya, the one with all the signatures. When Mrs. Fredericks is givin' us our pay, she has us signin' so she has proof we've been paid, and it kapes anyone gettin' paid twice. Mrs. Fitzgerald's name isn't on it. Her name is on the list of people who *need* ta be paid, but 'tis not on the paper sayin' she actually *was* paid."

"So? What does that mean?"

"That means the bookkapeer's sendin' pay fer her, an' she never signs sayin' that she received any. So I knew that someone had her money."

"So what you're saying is, the person in charge of the money thinks Mrs. Fitzgerald is working here, so he sends her earnings every week. But since she doesn't really work here, she doesn't pick up her money or sign for it…"

"An' someone has ta be takin' that leftover money," Anna said smugly.

"You're right," I mused. "Someone's keeping the money she's supposedly making."

Anna looked deep in thought. "I'm thinkin' we should be showin' this ta Reed's boss."

I sneezed suddenly.

"God's blessin' ta ya," she said.

"Thank you. Wait, Anna, I just had a terrible thought. What if there's another woman with the same name? I mean, there are a lot of ladies named Mary in the world. And if we take that to Mr. Reed's boss, we're going to look pretty silly."

"Hmm, 'tis true enough. An' with so many Irish immigrants 'round here, Fitzgerald might not be that uncommon.

How can we possibly be findin' out if there 'tis another Mary Fitzgerald that's workin' here?"

I shrugged. "I have no idea where to even begin to find out something like that."

Anna folded the papers and put them in her apron pocket so we could get back to the vats. "I've got ta be findin' out if there is another workin' here who has the same name," she fumed. "Could be a coincidence, ta be sure, but if 'twere, why would she be on Reed's list, but not on the signature list? Why is the bookkapeer thinkin' she's in this area? Mary Smith 'tis the only Mary I know 'round our area."

"Hmm, good point." I sneezed again.

"God love ya. Are ya feelin' all right?"

"Thank you, and yes, I'm fine."

I leaned away from the fresh chicken and sneezed once more. "I'm just sneezing because it's a bit chilly in here."

Anna looked doubtful. "Ya go take a break. I'll take care o' catchin' up the chickens."

"All right," I told her. I went down to the restroom to blow my nose, then sat down on one of the benches near our lockers. Over and over again I pondered how Mr. Reed got the bookkeepers to think Mrs. Fitzgerald was working here without being caught, and how we could possibly check to see if there was indeed another woman with the same name who just happened to be working in the factory.

I'm not sure what happened next, but I must've dozed off for a minute. I woke with a start, then stood up and headed back to work, feeling a little foolish, but also very tired.

When I got back to the vats, I asked, "Anna, how did you get those papers?"

"Remember this mornin' when yer Mum asked me ta let Mrs. Fredericks know that the trucks were in the loadin' docks?"

"Yes."

"While I was waitin' fer her, I wandered o'er ta look at that picture on her wall, an' I noticed somethin' stickin' out from behind the filin' cabinet. I grabbed these two sheets o' paper, an' ta be sure I was goin' ta put them on her desk, but I saw me name on them an' took a closer look. I realized 'twas just our pay sheets."

"Oh," I said. "So how did you notice Mrs. Fitzgerald's name?"

"I'm shamed ta say it. I could've put them on her desk, but 'twas just bein' nosy. I was wonderin' how much different folks make, an' I started readin' the paper. Next thing I know, I'm matchin' names an' signatures."

"And you didn't get caught?"

"I almost was, but luckily I put them in me pocket when I heard her comin' back."

I thought for a moment. "You know what this means, don't you?"

"What?"

"This means that Mrs. Fredericks is a part of this."

"Aye-yah," she sighed wearily.

"Do you think she'll miss them? The papers you found?"

She shrugged. "I din'nat think so. They were stuck behind the filin' cabinet. They apparently fell back there and were ne'er noticed. I barely saw them meself."

"Well, that's good," I said. "I wonder if those were the missing papers Mum asked us about, you know, back when we were pulling pranks on Mrs. Fredericks?"

"Could be," she mused.

The whistle blew and Anna put the chickens in the vats. I went to the benches and began pulling off my boots. It felt so good to get them off, because I was feeling too warm in them.

"Beth, are ya feelin' well?" Anna asked when she came back

"Sure," I said. "Why?"

She shrugged. "I'm not knowin fer sure, but ya look a touch pale."

"I'm just feeling a little warm."

"Hmm… Earlier ya were feelin' cold."

"Oh, yeah…" I said, as I was putting on my coat. "I guessed I warmed up."

"Tis a terrible cold snap outside," Anna said as she slipped on her gloves. "Ya'd best bundle up, or ya'll be catchin' yer death o' cold."

"Yes, and I thought we were in for a fairly warm winter," I giggled. "I'll see you tomorrow."

"Indeed ya will, an' tanight I'll be thinkin' o' a plan ta catch auld Reed in the act."

"Good," I said, and sneezed again. "Let me know what your plan is."

"O' course! I'm needin' me best buddy ta help me carry it out. See ya then." She waved as we started toward the doors.

I ran outside and caught up with Mum. She and I walked home in silence, not because of any spats, but because the sun had set and the icy February wind whipped around our heads and ears, making any discussion a chore.

It was such a relief to get out of the cold and into my nice, warm house. I quickly unwound my scarf, shrugged off my coat, and moved next to the blazing fire that Papa had already built in the fireplace. I stood for a while, thawing my hands and feet, trying to shake off the chill.

"How's my girl?" Papa asked as he entered the living room.

I sneezed. "I had a pretty good day," was all I would say. I knew I couldn't tell anyone about our suspicions about Mr. Reed. After all, we were only teenagers, and Mr. Reed was an adult.

I went into the kitchen where Papa was pouring tea for the three of us and started stirring the soup he had on the stove. Uncle Elton wouldn't have to leave for work until later at night, so he came in and joined us. I listened quietly as the adults talked.

"Beth?" Mum asked in concerned voice.

"Yes, ma'am?"

"Are ya all right? I asked ya twice ta bring me the sugar."

"Oh!" I said. "I guess I was just thinking about something else."

I put the sugar on the table and went back to get some bowls for the soup. Uncle Elton and Papa were discussing some store down the street that was going out of business, and Mum got everyone a glass of water.

Everyone sat down to eat, but I just sipped the broth. For some reason, it didn't taste right.

"Beth, is something wrong with your soup?" Papa asked.

"I don't know. It just doesn't taste good."

"Mine's fine," Mum said.

"Mine, too," Papa said.

"Mine as well," Uncle Elton chimed in.

I turned away and sneezed. "I guess I'm just not that hungry. May I go to bed and read?"

Mum gave me a peculiar look. "Sure, honey. Come give me a hug."

When I hugged her, Mum felt my forehead. "Beth! Yer burning up!"

"I am? Mum, I feel fine. I'm probably just hot from sitting next to the fire a little while ago."

She stood up and laid down her napkin. "Elizabeth, that isn't from a fire. Yer skin is actually hot, and I want ya ta sit down and eat a little of that soup. After that, I want ya ta go get inta bed. I'm going ta boil some water and put the hot water bottle in yer bed."

"Yes, ma'am," I said and sat back down. Papa reached over and felt my forehead as well.

"Your mum is right," Papa said. "You're burning up."

"Oh, Papa, I feel fine."

"Well, maybe we can stop this before it gets out of hand. I agree with your mother. Hurry up and eat and we'll get you to bed."

"Who's going to help you prepare the food to carry out to the homeless men?"

"I can help with that," Uncle Elton told me. "After all, I don't think they want ya makin' food fer them if yer sneezin' on it. Besides, with this cold snap, most of them are already in shelters fer the night."

"That's true," Papa said.

There was no easy way I could argue my way out of it, so I ate as much of my soup as I could handle, then I went on up to bed. I changed quickly, put on clean socks, and crawled into bed with the book I had received at Christmas. I was so disappointed that I wouldn't be able to stay up and listen to the radio with the rest of the family.

Within minutes, I was asleep and the next thing I knew, Mum was standing beside my bed, feeling my forehead.

"I'll be right down, Mum," I said, even though I was feeling pretty lousy.

"Oh, no ya won't," she said firmly. "Ya need ta stay in bed."

"Mum, I love you," I said jokingly, thinking that I wouldn't have to go to work. Suddenly, I remembered that Anna and I had planned to get together and find out if we were right about Mr. Reed stealing money, and sat up as quickly as I was able, feeling slightly dizzy.

"Mum, wait! I have to work today," I said, trying to sound as firm as she did, but failing. "I'll be fine, I promise." I struggled just trying to get out of bed.

"No, ma'am," she said, gently pushing me back into bed. "I want ya ta stay here and keep warm." Then she paused a moment, looking thoughtful. "Then again, maybe ya should get up. I think ya should move downstairs by the fireplace. The radiator in here won't keep ya as warm. Besides, yer father can keep a better eye on ya that way."

Seriously? The one day I actually wanted to go to work was the one day Mum wouldn't let me.

"But Mum," I started to argue, but I knew I would lose when she grabbed my pillow and headed out to the hall. She then got a blanket from the hall closet. "Come along, Beth. I want ta get ya situated before I leave."

"All right," I said, and I wobbled through the hall and down the stairs with just enough energy to make it to the sofa. By that time, I had stopped sneezing and had developed a deep cough that was leaving me breathless.

Scarcely moving from my spot all day, I slept most of the time from pure exhaustion when the cough allowed it. I managed to swallow a few spoonfuls of the soup Papa had heated up for lunch, but still had no appetite.

Even though I was feeling a bit better by the time Mum got home, I was still coughing and sneezing like crazy. "Well," she said calmly, "ya may feel better, but yer not going ta clean chickens with that sneezing and coughing."

"All right, Mum," I agreed.

"I'm going ta help yer father with dinner, so I'll be back in a minute."

She started to leave, she turned back to me, remembering something. "By the way, Anna said ta hurry back, because she 'found three more,' whatever that means."

For a split second, I was terrified. I thought I was going to have to explain what Anna had meant. Fortunately, she just smiled and walked into the kitchen.

My guess was Anna 'had found three more' papers with Mrs. Fitzgerald's name on them. If that was indeed what she meant, then there were at least three more times that Mrs. Fitzgerald was added to the list of people to be paid.

I couldn't wait to get to work the next day to find out, but Mum wouldn't let me go that day either. I waited all day long for Mum to get home so she could tell me what else Anna had said. Instead, she brought me a bundle of material tied with a pink ribbon.

"What's this?" I asked Mum when she gave it to me.

"Well, Anna gave it ta me and asked me ta ask ya if ya could sew her an apron fer her hope chest. I guess she wants one just like the one ya made me fer Christmas. She wanted ta know what ya thought of this material. Personally, I think it would be perfect fer Anna." With that, she turned and went into the kitchen to say hi to Papa.

I turned the material over and over in my lap and wondered why she would have sent it to me. I thought back to the Fourth of July picnic. We had discussed the fact that I couldn't sew and she couldn't cook. She knew I hated sewing, and I knew she had been sewing for years. Why would she ask me to make something for her?

Then, underneath a fold of material, I found a letter in an envelope.

She was so smart! She had thought of a way to get me a message without Mum realizing we were up to something.

I opened the letter and read it. She said she had snuck into Mrs. Frederick's office, looked through the file cabinet and found several more pay sheets with Mrs. Fitzgerald's name on them. She also said she had found out that there were only a few Mrs. Fitzgerald's at our plant, and none of them were named Mary.

I was thrilled. I knew we were on the right track. I grew even more excited to get to work the next day.

Mum, however, had other ideas. "No," she said flatly. "I don't want ya ta go out inta that cold until ya've been without a fever fer one whole day."

"Fine," I muttered. I hid the note in my top dresser drawer and stayed in bed for a third day. I was bored stiff.

I waited in bed for the long, boring day to end. I read several chapters in my book and wrote a note back to Anna. I heard some scurrying around downstairs, but I kept reading. Then there was a knock at the front door, and I called down to Papa to answer it.

"I have it!" he called back. I went back to bed and took my temperature again. There was no more fever, so I was sure that Mum would let me go back to work the next day. She just had to. I was dying to help Anna with one of her plans and didn't think I could take one more day cooped up in the house.

There was a knock at my door. "Come in, Papa."

"'Tis me, Beth," Aunt Martha said.

"Well, this is nice. What are you doing here?"

"Oh, I was just bringin' up some tea fer ya," she said, as she handed me a cup and saucer. "How are ya feelin'?"

"Much better," I told her. "I can't wait to get back to work. I'm going nuts having to stay in bed."

Aunt Martha's smile was forced. I could tell something was wrong.

"Aunt Martha, is something bothering you?"

"'Tis nothin'. I'm just concerned, and wantin' ta make sure yer all right."

"I'm fine," I assured her. I sipped the tea gingerly. It was warm and soothing on such a cold day. We talked for a couple of minutes, and as soon as I finished my tea, she took the cup from me.

"Beth, yer mum needs ta talk ta ya," she said suddenly.

"Well, now that you have me curious, I don't think I can wait until she gets home. Maybe you could go ahead and tell me what it's about."

"She is home," Aunt Martha said.

That was when I knew something was desperately wrong. It was only three o'clock and Mum wouldn't be home unless it was really important.

CHAPTER SEVENTEEN

In Shock

"What's wrong? Is it Dale?" I pushed my covers off to go downstairs.

"No, Beth. Get back in bed. Nothin's wrong with Dale."

"Then what?" I asked, ignoring her instructions to stay in bed, and swinging my feet off the side.

"Beth, she wants ta talk ta ya here," she started out, trying to push me back to my bed.

"But what's wrong?" I practically screamed.

The door opened. We both froze. Mum was standing there, looking tired and anxious.

"Mum, what's wrong?"

Mum stepped over and gently pushed me back to the bed, placed the covers over me, and sat on the edge of my bed. Aunt Martha moved to the door, looking like she did the day Dale left. I was so scared I didn't fight them anymore.

"Beth," Mum said gently, taking my hands in hers. "It's Anna."

All I could think was, "Oh, no, she's been caught!" I just knew we were in trouble.

"Honey, there's been an accident."

"What?" There was a burning in the pit of my stomach.

"She's… she's dead."

"What?"

"Ya know, it's been very cold outside. Taday, fer some reason," Mum's voice broke slightly, "she was over in packaging. The factory was very cold. She was wearing her coat, the big furry one. I don't quite know what happened. She was standing…"

"No," I interrupted quietly.

"She was standing next ta a box grinder."

"No." I repeated, slightly louder.

"It grabbed her coat."

"*No!*" My voice was rising in pain and denial.

"It pulled her inta the grinder before anyone could get her out."

"NO!!" The burning was consuming my whole body. I fought to get out of the bed. "Anna! Anna!"

I wanted to run down to the factory, to see it for myself. I wanted to show them that it was all a mistake. Anna was fine. There had to be a mistake. It wasn't her!

"Anna!" I tried to run down there, but they held me and murmured to me, until my hysterical screams turned to violent sobs. My fighting against them grew less and less, and I realized they must have put some sort of sleeping powder in my tea. They pulled me back into the bed, and I saw Papa standing at the door, looking sorrowful. I tried one more time to get up, but it was pointless. The powder was beginning to work, and all I could do was realize, truly realize, how much I hated that place.

Suddenly, I knew it was true. She was gone.

My best friend in the whole world was gone.

Later that night, when I woke up, I knew it was true. Anna was dead. I stayed in my bed and cried. I wept until my pillow was soaked through and I was exhausted.

Wearily, I got up, put on my housecoat and slippers and went downstairs. Mum was in the kitchen cleaning up the dinner dishes, but I didn't see Papa. I looked at the clock, and it was almost 8:00. I thought he was probably out helping the homeless men.

Aunt Martha wasn't around either. She must've gone back home.

Mum came over and put her arms around me. "Beth, are ya all right?"

I brushed her aside and sat down at the table. "I'm fine," I said.

"Do ya want anything ta eat?"

"No, thank you."

She poured me some tea anyway, and then finished putting away the dinner dishes. I sat in silence for a long time, just staring at the cup.

"When is the funeral?" I asked finally. My voice sounded raspy from my earlier outburst.

"Tamorrow," she said. "I know yer feeling better. Do ya want ta go?"

"Of course." How could she not think I would want to go?

"I'll be going, and so will the other ladies in my area."

"Can we afford for you to miss work tomorrow?"

Mum sat down and stirred her own tea. "The factory was shut down taday... just after it happened. It'll be shut down tamorrow as well. We're not expected ta return ta work until Monday."

I poured some sugar into my tea, and the tears started pouring down my face again. They were not the angry, violent tears from the early afternoon. These were tears of loss.

Mum came over and put her arms around me while I cried.

"Oh, Mum, how could something like this happen? Why was she in that area? Why did it have to happen?"

She began rocking me back and forth in her arms. "I don't know, me dear. I just don't know. And they wouldn't let us inta the area. I'm so sorry. I just know Mr. Reed did everything he could ta get ta her before the machine did."

"Mr. Reed?!" I screamed, pulling away from her. "Mr. Reed was there? He did this?"

"No, no, no me darling. He didn't do this. I'm sure he did everything he could ta prevent it."

"No!" I jumped up from my chair. "He did this! I know he did this!"

"Darling," she raised her voice, only in an attempt to be heard, "I know ya don't like Mr. Reed, but he can't be blamed. It was an accident…"

I was already halfway up the stairs. I didn't believe her. I knew he had something to do with Anna's death. All I needed was some way to prove it.

The day of the funeral dawned overcast and cold, perfectly suiting my feelings. I chose my nicest gray dress to wear, as it was the closest thing I had to black. I moved through the morning in a daze, unable to eat, think or even cry. I felt completely numb inside. Mum and I made our way inside the church from the bitter cold, blustery day. It was packed with people. Practically everyone from the factory was there, including Mr. Reed. When I saw him, the numbness inside me turned to seething rage. I wanted to leap out of my seat and scream at him, letting everyone present know this was his fault. I wanted to run over and pummel him with my fists, causing him pain as he had caused me pain.

The only problem was I didn't have the nerve.

My gaze turned back towards the closed coffin, and I wished I could see Anna one more time. I'd have given anything to hear her laugh or see her eyes sparkle with mischief and fun just once more.

Looking around the crowded church, I saw Anna's fiancé, sitting with two older people who I assumed were Anna's parents. The three of them clung tightly to one another, and Fred appeared to be trying to hold himself together, but when the priest stepped up into the pulpit to begin the service, Fred dropped his head to the woman's shoulder and began crying like a baby. The dam broke inside me at the sight of his grief, and I put my head upon my own mum's shoulder and wept. She handed me her handkerchief, and I tried to wipe the tears from my eyes, but they flowed too quickly.

The priest began the service, but I couldn't concentrate on what he was saying. He talked about Anna's short life, her laugh, and her warm and caring personality. He obviously knew her well. Then he began reciting Anna's favorite Bible passage, the 23rd Psalm. When he got to the part that said, "Yea, though I walk through the valley of the shadow of death, I will fear no evil," I started staring at Mr. Reed.

Deep in my heart, I knew Mr. Reed was the reason Anna died. I didn't know how he was to blame, but I was sure it was his fault.

After the service, we followed the others to Anna's parent's house for the reception. Everyone talked in hushed tones about how nice the service was, and I heard bits and pieces of stories of Anna's life before I knew her. Any other time, I would've loved to hear them, but at the moment, I felt bone weary and a bit detached from everything around me.

As I sat quietly in a corner, I heard my name. "Beth?"

"Yes?" I looked up to see Fred standing beside me. I hadn't even heard him approach.

"I thought that was you," he said. "I wanted to give something to you. Something that Anna would've wanted you to have."

I stood up. "What?"

He held out a small package, his hands trembling as he spoke. "Anna was going to wear these at our wedding. She had just bought them."

"What are they?"

He opened the box, pulling away the tissue paper, showing me two hand-carved hair combs with an intricate design on them. They were incredibly beautiful.

I was floored. "Fred...I... I can't take these," I told him.

His voice started shaking, and tears flowed from his eyes. "She told me that one day she wanted to give them to you for your wedding, something you'd both be able to share. She said you were the best friend she'd ever had, even though you were younger than her. That's how I know she'd want you to have them."

Still I hesitated. They were obviously expensive. *She must've saved forever to buy them.*

He caught my hand in his own, gently placing the box on my palm. "Please?" His heartbroken tone shattered my last doubt, and I stared at the beautiful combs and thought about how lovely she would have looked with them holding back her long, red hair.

"Thank you, Fred. I promise to take good care of them and treasure them always." My voice broke as well.

"Thank you," he choked out, hugging me for a moment, then disappearing into the crowd.

I never saw him again.

Soon after, Mum came over and said it was time to go. I showed her the combs and told her what Fred had said. She looked sad, but gave me a warm hug. I grabbed my coat, gave my condolences to Anna's parents, and headed outside. I waited on the porch for Mum, the cold wind blistering my hands and face, but I didn't care. It seemed far too warm and crowded inside the house, and my head felt strange. After several minutes, Mum joined me, and we trudged home silently. It seemed to take forever to get there, and I was shivering by the time we arrived. Mum looked at me with concern. "I hope ya didn't go out in the cold too soon after just starting ta get well."

I shook my head. "No, I'm fine. Just tired and a little cold."

"Hmmm...I think it's a hot bath and bed fer ya, young lady."

"Oh, Mum..." In truth that sounded heavenly, but I didn't want to act like I was feeling ill again.

"Don't ya 'oh Mum' me, now. Scoot upstairs and get inta yer housecoat, and I'll get a bath ready."

By the time I'd changed and come back downstairs, Mum had the washtub from the basement filled with hot water and had started some tea as well. I slipped into the wonderful warmth, as she went upstairs to change her own clothes. I almost fell asleep in the tub, it felt so good, but Mum came back into the kitchen and roused me, helping me get into my nightclothes, as I just couldn't seem to manage them alone.

"Now drink this tea, and then we'll get ya ta bed."

I drank it all, then she helped me up the stairs and into bed. I was barely aware of her tucking me in and placing a cool palm against my forehead before darkness took me.

I don't remember much after that. There was a blur of sleep, faces, light and darkness, moments of heat so bad I squirmed and moments of being so cold I shivered. And I had the strangest dreams.

In one of them, I was sure I heard Mr. Reed and Mrs. Fredericks talking, right in my room. "I found it," Mr. Reed said, in a low but triumphant tone.

"Are you certain?" Mrs. Fredericks asked. She sounded anxious.

"I think so. As long as the girl doesn't talk, we'll be ok," Mr. Reed told her smugly.

"Anna's gone now, and this one doesn't worry me," Mrs. Fredericks replied, her voice calmer.

"She might talk. Maybe we better make sure she doesn't," he said, his voice moving closer. All of a sudden, something covered my face, pressing down hard. I gasped for breath, and but couldn't get any air. It was hot, which made me cough and then it became even harder to breathe. I choked and gagged, trying to lift my hands up to push away whatever it was, but felt myself get weaker and weaker. Then, as suddenly as it began, it ended. As my strange dream continued, Mrs. Fredericks grew angry with Mr. Reed. "Anna was an accident, but I will not stoop to letting you cause another death." Their voices seemed to move away slowly.

I coughed and coughed, and then everything faded to black as I heard a man say, "There's a fifty-fifty chance." Finally, I slept comfortably, and didn't have any more weird dreams.

I opened my eyes. A pinkish hue lit the room, so I figured it was evening, and the air was cool. The house was quiet, and Mum was asleep in the chair next to my bed. I got out of bed and gave her a kiss on the cheek. She never even moved, so I figured she was exhausted and decided to let her sleep.

I went to the restroom, then downstairs to get a cup of tea. The kitchen was full of people. Papa was there, talking with Aunt Martha and Uncle Randall, while Uncle Elton and Dr. Viosca were all standing near the stove.

"Hi," I said, and everyone got quiet. Then, with a sudden burst of energy, each person began talking at once.

"Beth!" Papa shouted, and everyone came running over to hug me.

"Goodness, young lady, you gave us quite a scare," Dr. Viosca said. "We thought we were going to have another funeral around here."

"Me dear, let me get ya a cup of tea," Aunt Martha said, wiping tears from her eyes.

"And some toasted bread," Dr. Viosca added. Then he turned and looked at me. "My son's going to be glad that you're awake. He's been asking about you."

"Really? Tommy's been asking about me?"

"Yes," Papa said. "He's come over three times."

"He sure has," Dr. Viosca chuckled. "Now, you need to get back to bed, young lady. I'll have your aunt bring your tea and toast, and when I get home, I'll let Tomic know you're awake. He'll be glad to hear it."

"Where's yer mum?" Uncle Elton asked.

"She's upstairs asleep," I told him.

"Then let's go see her," Uncle Randall said. "And I'll help ya back ta bed."

"I'll bring her some tea as well," Aunt Martha said, pulling out the tea canister.

Papa swept me up in his strong arms and carried me back to bed.

"Margaret!" Papa started calling as soon as we got to my room. "It's over! Honey, she's awake!"

Mum jumped. "What?" she said with a start.

"She's awake!" Papa repeated.

Mum looked at me. Then she came over, put her arms around me, and began crying. "Oh, me baby," she kept repeating. "Me baby girl."

Finally, she stopped crying, and Dr. Viosca insisted that we both go to bed.

"Ya put Margaret ta bed," Aunt Martha said to Papa. "I'll take care of this one."

"All right," he agreed. "Come along, sweetheart. The worst is over."

Mum smiled, hugged me again, and then went to her own room. Dr. Viosca followed them out, and Uncle Randall headed back downstairs, leaving me and Aunt Martha alone to talk.

"Yer mum needs her rest," Aunt Martha told me as she helped me get under the covers. "She's been with ya almost constantly."

"I bet she is tired," I said. "With that funeral yesterday, and having to sit up all night with me..."

"Yesterday?" Aunt Martha said. "Honey, the funeral was Friday. 'Tis Tuesday."

"What? How long was I asleep?"

"Since Friday night, I think. She called me over on Saturday."

"Good grief," I said. "So that means I've been asleep for... three days?"

"Almost four. We were really worried. Dr. Viosca said ya have pneumonia."

"Pneumonia?" I sat back in my pillows. "No wonder everyone was acting so strangely."

She poured the tea and sat on the bed. "Several people have been over ta visit ya. That boy, Tommy, came by, and then there was some little girl ya went ta school with, some people from church, some people from work."

"Tommy? Really?" I almost squealed. No wonder they said he'd been here three times.

"Aye-yah," she said, as she poured tea. "He's quite a nice young man. A friend of yer brother's, I believe."

"Yes, he is. And what friend from school?"

"Hmm. What was her name? Allison, I think. "

"Oh, yes, I know Allison." I felt happy that so many people were worried about me. Then I realized something else she had said.

"Wait. People from work? They were here?"

"I think so. Yer mum said 'twas a boss an' some other lady. I don't remember what their names were. She could probably tell ya."

I began to tremble. "Was it Mr. Reed?"

"I don't remember," she repeated. "Like I said, ya'd have ta ask yer mum."

Of Chickens and Hobos

Even though I knew there was no way Mum would allow a grown man into my room while I was asleep, I couldn't help but think of the strange dream I had about Mrs. Fredericks and Mr. Reed being in my room. I jumped up and went to my top drawer of my dresser.

"Me dear, what are ya doin'? Ya should be in bed!" Aunt Martha told me.

The letters from Anna were still hidden behind my socks, just where I'd left them on the day of the funeral. In my dream, Mr. Reed had been looking for something, so knowing they were there brought a wave of relief over me, and I could calm down and get back into bed.

So it really was just a dream, right?

I mean, surely it was just a dream. Right?

CHAPTER EIGHTEEN
My Own Business

It was two more weeks before Dr. Viosca said I was well enough to go back to work, but by then Mrs. Fredericks had already replaced both Anna and me. I didn't really care because I hated that place, and I was afraid to go back anyways.

Besides, without Anna there, it wouldn't be the same. It hurt just to think about it.

Even though I was thrilled about not having to go back to that place, I started worrying about the money. I thought Mum would too, but she seemed relieved. She didn't want me to go back, either, after "the incident." She still thought it was an accident, but I knew better. I just didn't have any way to prove it.

Papa had found a week-long job, and Uncle Elton was bringing in money, so I guess she wasn't as worried about it as I was. I didn't want to lie around the house though. I thought about going back to school, but it was March, so school would be out soon for the summer anyway. Maybe I'd go back in the fall when the new semester started.

I decided the best way I could help out was to do the house cleaning and laundry. Since Mum and Papa were working, and Uncle Elton was asleep during the day, I was free to do as I wanted.

One morning, I started by doing Mum's spring cleaning in the kitchen. I cleaned out the cabinets, pantries, and drawers, then scrubbed them all. After that, I cleaned the lamps, scrubbed the baseboards, swept, mopped, and waxed the floor. I had just enough time to start dinner before Mum got home.

I was so proud of the way Mum reacted when she arrived. She was thrilled.

"Elizabeth, this is wonderful!" she exclaimed. "Everything is sparkling, the floors are spotless, and ya even did the baseboards! And what is this?" She lifted the lid off of the pot on the stove and sniffed at it. "Is this chicken and rice soup?"

"Yes," I said as nonchalantly as I could.

"Oh, my word, 'tis lovely. 'Tis cold out today, and this will just hit the spot. And it is so nice in here!" She went on and on, and then Papa came in and raved about the great job I did as well.

As much as I enjoyed the compliments and the feeling of pride, all the work did wear me out. I guess I was still tired from the pneumonia, so I did nothing the next day but read and cook dinner.

It was only a couple of days after that when Mum came home with some good news. "The ladies at work were asking how ya were doing. I told them about how ya were, and about what a fabulous job ya'd done on our kitchen, so one of them asked if ya'd be willing ta do her kitchen spring cleaning as well."

"Well, I don't know," I began. "I'm still tired from doing our kitchen."

"Oh, ya can pick any day ya want. She's offering ta pay ya a dollar, and she'll even give ya a dime for the bus ride home."

"A whole dollar? That's as much as I was making in a week at the factory!" I didn't really want to do another kitchen, but the money could definitely come in handy. And I knew adults got paid more than kids, so she could probably afford it better than I could have. An entire dollar?

"All right," I said. "When does she want me to come over?"

"I'll get the information from her at work tamorrow. I know she'll appreciate it."

The next evening, she came home and gave me a slip of paper with the address on it, and the following morning I presented myself at the woman's house. "I'm here," I announced when Mrs. Baker appeared at the door.

"So you are," she said, and she smiled, making me feel perfectly at ease. "I have some things here to help you out with your work. I've left some ham sandwiches and fruit for you in the ice box, and some milk if you would like it. I also have a record player if you'd like to use it to keep you company." She looked me over and said, "Are you sure you can stand being here alone all day?"

"I really don't mind," I told her politely. "And a record player? I'll be quite happy with that!"

"Good," she said pleasantly, "I'll be back this evening."

The second she left, I ran to the record player. I sorted through the records and took one out that looked like it would be a good selection. I carefully put the record on the small, circular table, then I turned the crank around and around, until the record began turning. I lowered the arm and the music began to play. I waltzed around, pretending that I was dancing with some young gentleman at some grand ball. I practiced a few Lindy Hop steps and a little Charleston. But after just a couple of songs, I realized I didn't have much time to play. I had a job to do, and if I wanted my dollar, I needed to get busy.

First, I cleaned out all of the food from the pantry and the dishes from the cabinets. I filled a bucket with hot, soapy water, and scrubbed and scrubbed until every shelf in the kitchen was clean. After that, I rearranged everything so that every bowl, plate, glass, and jar were easier to find. Next,

I cleaned out all of the drawers, scrubbed them down and continued working until the entire kitchen almost sparkled. The only time I stopped was to rewind the record player and to eat lunch. I scraped the floor and applied fresh, clean wax. At that point, I had another hour until Mrs. Baker was to return home. So I refilled the hot water bucket and washed the windows, finishing up just as she came through the door.

"Oh, Beth!" she gasped. "This is wonderful! I'm not so sure I could've done this for myself."

"Thank you," I said. I waited while she sifted through her things and pulled out a dollar. "This is for you, and here's a dime for the bus, just as I promised your mother. But this is especially for you." She handed me a string of licorice, the red kind, which is my favorite.

"Oh, that's just grand!" I said. "Thank you very much."

"I wish it could be more," she told me, "but you know how tough times are. I'd rather give you a dollar of your own to spend, but we just don't have the money right now."

"Don't worry, Mrs. Baker. This is fine. I haven't had a store-bought candy like this since Christmas. This is very nice."

She thanked me again and I hurried off to catch the bus home. I enjoyed half of my licorice string on the bus, and I gave the other half to a little boy who sat across from me. He looked like he was down on his luck, too. I'm pretty sure he hadn't had store-bought candy in a while either.

When I got home, Papa had a nice dinner waiting. After dinner, I spent the evening enjoying a good book. The next day, Mum came home and told me that Mrs. Baker was very happy with the way I had done my work. She'd been so impressed, that she told two other ladies, who asked if I would mind coming over to their houses to do the same for them. I agreed, and so I worked for the next two days. Within two weeks, I had several people lined up asking for my house cleaning services.

It was also pretty fun for me because I felt like I was running my own business. The work itself was hard, but

I loved not having to deal with whistles and cranky bosses looking over my shoulder the entire time. I could work at my own pace and not worry about having Mr. Reed or Mrs. Fredericks yell at me. I especially enjoyed not having to put up with Harold. The best part was that I didn't have to get up as early every morning as I did when I worked at the factory, and if I got done early, I could leave and still get my dollar. I was making up to five dollars a week, and sometimes more. That was far more than I'd made at the factory working longer hours.

It was really surprising how well I was doing. Papa even joked about how I should hire some help; then I could get twice the amount of work done.

One day, however, a lady stopped by the house and asked Mum if I could clean her house for a fancy party she was throwing. Mum accepted that job because she reasoned that if someone could afford to throw a fancy party, she might also offer to pay a little more for such a project.

I showed up early at Mrs. Moore's house. I walked up the long, winding drive, past the shrubs and flower beds and stopped for a moment to look at it. It wasn't a grand old house, like the types that had servants living with them, but it was nice. It was a large, newer home, with a beautiful front porch sporting white columns that reached up to the top of the second story of the house. Yes, these people seemed to have money.

I was hoping to really impress this lady so that maybe she'd tell some rich friends and they'd hire me as well. I was so excited when I knocked on the door, only to find it being opened by Sadie Moore.

Really? Sadie Moore? I hadn't even thought about the fact the lady's last name was Moore.

"Beth," she exclaimed. "I didn't know you were the working girl Mother had hired. Will you also be one of the serving girls on the night of Mother's party?"

Her words dripped with honey, yet didn't conceal her amusement at the fact I was the scullery maid for the day. I started to snap at her, but then I remembered the calm, sweet way Anna had handled her on the day of the picnic.

"No, I'm afraid I won't be there for your party," I said calmly.

"Oh, it's too bad you'll miss it," she cooed as she showed me the way to the kitchen. "It'll be a simply grand affair. Dr. and Mrs. Viosca will be there, so Tommy will probably come with them. It'll be just lovely."

"Well, that's unfortunate," I said, emulating Anna as best I could. "But my company only allows one enough time to clean kitchen areas, not to do catering."

"Your company?" she asked in obvious amusement.

"Yes, I'm 15 and in charge of my own business."

"Oh, how cute," she said. "A house cleaning business. How appropriate for a lower class child such as yourself."

I was so tired of her laughing at me, demeaning me every chance she got. I wanted to really tell her off, but by this time, we'd reached the kitchen, and Mrs. Moore was washing the breakfast dishes.

"Good, morning," she chirped merrily. I'd never met her before, and I was surprised to find that she was cheerful and welcoming. She didn't seem to have the air of arrogance that Sadie did.

"Thank you for coming," Mrs. Moore said pleasantly, as she began to give me a tour of the kitchen. "Let me show you around. I've placed all the cleaning supplies here by the table. Here are all of the cabinets, the glasses should go over here, and the dishes can be set up over here. Here's the pantry, but it's pretty large, so you may even need to finish working on it tomorrow. If you need to, I can pay you fifty cents more. Also, my daughter, Sadie, will be in and out of the house today, so if you have any questions, you can just ask her."

"All right, ma'am," I said.

"Do you think you can manage it?" She smiled at me.

I looked around the huge kitchen. For several minutes I opened cupboards, drawers and doors. I looked around. "Yes, ma'am," I assured her. "I can do the job, but you're right about one thing. It may take me two days if every single cabinet needs to be scrubbed."

"It's a deal," Mrs. Moore said. She stretched out her hand. I paused a moment, then shook hands with her. Unlike Sadie, Mrs. Moore treated me with respect, just like I was any other adult. I really appreciated that about her, and it made me want to do an even better job.

"Good. Now, here are some sandwiches, fruit, milk, and fresh cookies for your lunch. I hope you don't mind that for your meal?"

"Oh, no ma'am. I never mind fresh cookies," I laughed.

She gave me a warm smile. "Well, I'm glad. We'll go and get out of your way, and I'll see you this afternoon. Come along, Sadie."

Sadie gave me a smug look, then she left with her mother. I was glad she was gone. I sat at the table and looked around the large kitchen for several minutes as I planned my cleaning strategy, then threw myself into my work.

I worked fast and furiously, determined to show everyone what a good worker I was, and to show Sadie that I could be mature about it. I just knew Anna would've been proud of my efforts.

By lunchtime, I'd completely finished what would be the hardest part of the work- the pantry. I'd emptied it, scrubbed it from top to bottom, and put the contents back inside in a more organized fashion. Then I got my lunch from the ice box and made myself a little picnic on the floor. I sat down and rested next to the warm radiator. It was the first break I'd taken all morning.

"What's this?" came a shrill voice from behind me. I jumped from the surprise of finding Sadie at the doorway. "My mother's paying you good money, and here you sit on your lazy behind. Get to work, scullery maid, or I'll let my mother know about this."

I wasn't finished with my lunch, but I couldn't afford to lose any of my money, or my possible customers, so I grudgingly stood up. I took my plate off the floor and replaced it in the icebox. I bit my tongue as I refilled the bucket of soapy water. Sadie sat there, watching me in the same way Mrs. Fredericks used to do.

It wasn't until I'd climbed up onto a stool to clean out the first cabinet before she decided to quit watching and make her own lunch. She sliced bread and ham for sandwiches, then cut some fruit and started a pot of tea. I hummed quietly to help keep my mind off her.

I thought I'd wait until she left to finish my lunch, but as soon as she had finished preparing her own, she made an unexpected announcement.

"Girl, I'm having some friends over for lunch, and I'll expect you to help and remain here in the kitchen. And try not to make any noise. We'll be trying to relax." I started to tell her she'd wasted her breath since I didn't even want to be in the same room with her, but I kept silent.

There was a knock at the front door and Sadie disappeared. It was a relief to have her gone. I started to go back to get my food, but she came back in, so I kept right on working. She left again, and I could hear her in the other room, laughing and talking with her friends.

I thought perhaps having her friends over would keep her occupied so that she'd leave me alone, but after a few minutes she popped her head in the door.

"You, come over here, now," she said snidely, and then went into the other room.

I climbed off the stool I was using and washed my hands, curious as to what she wanted. I entered the dining room. Sadie sat at the table with two other girls. They all turned and looked at me with distaste. I felt extremely uncomfortable.

I was wearing an old apron covered in dust and grime. They were all sitting at the dining table wearing pretty, clean, and what looked like new dresses.

"Yes ma'am?" I asked.

"Girl, we're ready for our tea," she said.

I stood there, puzzled. "What?" I said, blinking a bit.

"We're ready for the tea," she repeated coolly. One of the girls giggled a bit.

"Well," I ventured, "It's ready."

"Good," she said. "Then bring it in the good cups."

Still confused, I looked around. "The good cups?" I repeated.

Rolling her eyes, Sadie stood up. "I'm so sorry," she said to her friends. "I'll be right back." Then she took me by the hand and jerked me into the kitchen. She reached up and took a pink teacup from the cabinet and thrust it at me.

"These are the good cups and there's the teapot. Now hurry and bring the tea. The platter is right there."

"Wait a minute," I said, realizing what she wanted. "Your mum said that…"

"She said that you were to listen to me," she seethed.

"She said I could ask you questions," I corrected, trying not to snap at her.

She smiled. "Well, you asked which were the good cups, so I'm telling you the ones to use. And if you don't," she said, as she got very quiet and leaned in close to my face, "I'll tell my mother how you were sitting down on the job when you should've been working. You don't want that, do you? Or do you want to go back to the chicken factory?"

Every muscle in my body tensed. I was furious. She had me. If I lost business because of her, would I have to go back to the factory? I hated that thought.

I took a teacup from her hand and grabbed two more. With a triumphant smile, Sadie left the room. I placed the cups on the tray and poured the tea. Tears welled up in my eyes, but I carried the tray out to them with as much dignity as I could manage. I vowed that I wouldn't let them see me cry.

I served the tea quickly so I wouldn't have to look them in the eyes. I was almost out of the dining room when Sadie snapped her fingers. "Girl? You can serve the luncheon now."

"Yes, ma'am," I said. I wanted to scream and hit her, but brought back the sandwiches, fruit, and cookies, so for a while they left me alone. By that time, I'd lost my appetite, so I didn't even bother getting my own sandwiches out again. I went back to working on the kitchen.

"Girl?" Sadie called a bit later, about the time I thought she was through tormenting me.

I dropped what I was working on and went into the dining room. "Yes?"

"We are leaving now. You may take the luncheon tray."

Playing the part of the good servant, I went to the table and picked up all the dishes. I stood in icy silence, glaring at her when she smiled and waved goodbye as they left. I grabbed the tray, cleared off the table, and return to the kitchen. It was only then that I realized she had left her mess for me to clean up in addition to the work her mother had hired me to do.

By that time, I was beyond furious, and was behind on the work I'd been actually hired to do. I wanted to leave, but I certainly didn't want to go back there the next day, so I began cleaning with a new fury. My only goal was to leave that house and to prove I could do my job first.

I scrubbed the floors and baseboards, and then I cleaned the floors by hand. They weren't wood, so I didn't have to wax them. In no time I was finished.

I was thinking that maybe Mrs. Moore could give a good recommendation for me later, so I was determined to do the best job humanly possible. Plus, it was getting late, and she still wasn't home, so I decided to pour a new bucket of water and wash the windows as I'd done for Mrs. Baker.

It was getting almost dark by the time I finished, but everything looked great. I hoped Mrs. Moore would think so, but she hadn't come home yet. I put away the cleaning supplies and had just sat down at the table to drink the rest of the milk I had left over from lunch when Sadie entered.

"My mother called and told me that she'd be getting back later than she thought. She said I was to pay you," she told me. It added insult to injury, but I stood up and waited. I just wanted to get my dollar and leave.

"Hmm." Sadie looked around at the counters and snooped through the cupboards, then examined the pantry. "Well, here's your dollars' worth of change, and I believe mother said I was to also give you an extra dime."

I said nothing, but I took the coins and grabbed my apron to leave.

"You know," she said, "I was really expecting a lot more for a dollar, but I suppose you can't expect that much out of a child."

That's when it happened.

I snapped.

CHAPTER NINETEEN
What Goes Around...

She'd made one insult too many. Before I even realized what I was doing, I spun around on my heel and threw the coins at her as hard as I could.

"Here!" I screamed. "Take it! It might not buy a clean enough kitchen for you, but maybe you can take it and buy some good manners! My family might be poor, but at least we have manners!"

Turning my back to her, I stormed out of the house, accompanied by the sound of bouncing coins filling the air.

Never in my life had I yelled at someone like that, but at the moment, I didn't care. I was sick of being bullied. Sadie did it every chance she got; Mrs. Fredericks had been no better, and Mr. Reed was just downright abusive. I'd lost my best friend, my brother, and an entire year of school. To top it all off, I'd just lost my dollar, and my dime.

What was I going to say to Mum?

Then, as if I deserved one more slap in the face, it occurred to me that I'd have to walk home instead of taking the bus. I hated everything in life at that moment. It seemed the only good things I had in my life right now were my mum and papa, and I'd just been bullied out of the money I was going to give them. Just how angry was my mum going to be?

I hadn't realized I was crying until that moment. I'd been so full of anger that it felt good to let it out. Since I was facing a long walk home anyhow, I let the tears flow freely. Several people with cars stopped and asked me if I wanted a ride, but I told them all, "No, thank you," without looking at them. I didn't feel like explaining things to anyone.

But then, from one of the cars, came some startling words. "Beth, I don't think you should be walking home if you're this upset."

Stunned that anyone on that side of town would even know my name, I stopped and looked to see who it was. I was horrified.

It was Tommy.

I can't let me him see me crying like a baby! I thought to myself, and I started to run away, but that seemed even more babyish, so I turned around and faced him instead.

"Oh, my word, Beth," he said, getting out of his car and coming around to meet me. "What's happened?"

"Oh... it's just that, well, I..." I couldn't tell him about Sadie. She was his girlfriend. I decided the best thing to do was gloss over the truth. "It's just something about work," I told him.

"Well here, let me give you a ride," he offered, opening the car door for me. "I'm old enough to drive my father's car now."

"I know," I told him as I took a seat. "I saw you."

He looked surprised. "You did? When?" He started the car and we drove off down the street.

"I saw you last fall; October, I think it was. You were driving around with a girl," I muttered. I sniffled a little at the thought, because the girl I'd seen him with had been Sadie, of course, and I was so mad at her I couldn't say her name.

He smiled. "I don't remember that, but I'm more than happy to have you in the car with me. Now tell me what happened."

I stared out the window, into the dark, not really hearing the compliment he'd given me. "I don't want to tell you."

"Was it someone at the factory? I heard what happened to your friend. The one I met at the picnic, right?"

"Yes, you did, but no. It had nothing to do with the factory. I don't work there anymore."

"Really?" He seemed genuinely interested. "So, where were you?"

I sighed heavily. "I work cleaning kitchens for women, to help them out with their spring cleaning."

"And who's your boss?" he asked.

"Me. And whoever I work for that day."

"Wow! You mean you're your own boss? That's great."

"Well, yes," I blushed.

"I'm impressed," he said. "So you're angry with your boss, which is you. So what did you do that made you so upset?"

I looked away again, suddenly trying not to laugh. "I lost my temper and threw some money at someone."

"What?"

"The lady I was cleaning for has a daughter, and she came home as I was eating lunch. She said if I didn't do what she told me to do, she would tell her mom that I was sitting down on the job."

"You're kidding," he said, keeping his eyes on the road. The next thing I knew, I'd told him the whole story, but I didn't have the nerve to tell him it was Sadie who'd been so rude to me.

"Now what am I going to tell my mum?" I asked him at the end, tears creeping back into my eyes.

"Seems to me you should tell her the truth," he said thoughtfully. "Well, I might leave out the part where you told her to buy some manners. Although," he chuckled, "I would've loved to have seen that."

We sat in silence for several minutes. As we pulled up in front of my house, and he stopped the car, Tommy turned to me, placing his hand near mine.

"Beth, I know you had a bad day, but still, I'm proud of you. You stood up for yourself, and you don't do that very often. I think Dale would be proud of that too."

"Really?"

"Yes," he said. "I also think your family should be proud of the fact that when you lost your job, you started working for yourself. You didn't fall apart and cry. You went out and made the best of the situation. That's what impresses me the most about you."

I was stunned. "Thank you," I said, feeling a little embarrassed he'd caught me crying today.

"Do you want me to go inside with you to talk to your mum?"

"No," I said. "I think that if Dale was proud of me for acting like an adult, then I need to be adult enough to tell Mum what happened."

He smiled at me, and I just about melted as I stared into those brown eyes. "All right, but let me know what she says."

"I will," I told him. "Thank you for the ride home."

"You're welcome," he said. "You deserved it. You had a bad day."

I waved as Tommy drove off, then turned and marched into the house.

"Mum?" I called as I opened the door. I didn't know what I was going to say, but she had to be told. "Mum?"

"I'm in the kitchen," she called cheerfully.

I walked to the doorway and took a deep breath. "Mum, I have something to tell you."

"Gracious, Beth!" she exclaimed when she saw me. "What's happened ta ya?"

"Mum, I don't have any money to bring home today," I stated bluntly.

"Beth, what happened?" she asked again, fear creeping into the question.

I looked down and realized why she was asking. I was a complete mess. My hands were covered in blisters, my dress was wet and stained, my apron was wrapped around my arm, and my legs were scratched up from where I'd walked past some rosebushes before Tommy picked me up. I didn't even want to think about what my face must've looked like.

"Mum," I repeated, thinking she hadn't heard the part about the money, "I don't have any money today."

"Were ya robbed?" she asked, horrified, taking my hands.

"No, ma'am. I just don't have it." A few tears slipped down my face.

"It's okay, me dear. It'll be all right," she soothed, and wrapped me in a hug. In Mum's arms, I felt a new wave of tears spill from me. Then, almost in one long breath, I told her the whole story. I even ignored Tommy's advice and told her how I threw the money at Sadie.

"Mrs. Moore was really nice," I explained brokenly, between sobs, "and I wanted her to tell her rich friends about me, so I served the tea, but Sadie had the nerve to say I should've done more. Mum, I'm so sorry."

Mum held me and let me get it all out of my system. "Did ya do yer best?" she asked.

"Yes, ma'am, but..."

"Then ya don't owe anyone an apology," she told me firmly, then her face clouded. "If anything, that little snip owes ya an apology. After ya did all that hard work, she had the nerve ta ask ya ta serve her and her snooty friends! Just ta think of it makes me mad. They don't deserve the likes of ya, me darling."

And I'd been afraid Mum would be mad at me! She looked angry enough to wring Sadie's neck at the moment. She breathed heavily for several minutes, pacing rapidly about the kitchen, then let herself relax, smoothing away the angry expression she wore. Her voice gentled again. "Let's take a look at those hands." She gave me a tight hug and went to the pantry. I looked down at my hands. I'd not realized just how bad they looked and felt. They were red, and completely torn up. "Good grief, what did I do to them?"

Mum chuckled. "It looks like ya used water that was too hot again, but I've no idea how ya scraped them. And look at those bruises on yer arms. Ya really need ta be more careful."

We sat at the table and talked. Mum served tea and cookies, and cleaned my scratches, then rubbed petroleum jelly on my arms. She wrapped my arms with soft bandages and told me I didn't need to help with dinner or dishes that night. Her love and comfort melted the sour mood I was in. It was the first time I'd felt this relaxed in many months.

Papa got home late, and by the time we had dinner, it was getting to be late evening, so we were startled to hear a knock at the door. Papa left the table to answer the door and returned with a surprise announcement.

"It's Mrs. Moore," he said. "I think she wants to talk to the two of you."

I looked at Mum, and her body was tense, her expression angry.

"Really?" she asked as her eyes narrowed. "I'd like ta talk ta her as well." She walked briskly to the door and I followed. Papa put a hand gently on each of our shoulders, offering support and a sense of security.

"Mrs. Sundo," Mrs. Moore began. I thought she was going to ask Mum for permission to yell at me, which wouldn't have gone well. But instead, she said, "I believe my daughter owes your daughter an apology." I could barely see Sadie standing behind her mother, her eyes on her feet.

"Beg pardon?" I asked, unable to believe my ears. I felt Mum begin to relax beside me.

"Yes. She told me how you'd thrown the money at her, and when I got down to the bottom of it, I told her I didn't blame you. I would've thrown it as well." Mrs. Moore turned a withering stare to Sadie, who seemed to find her shoes extremely interesting at the moment. "Elizabeth, Mrs. Sundo, Mr. Sundo, I looked at that kitchen, and knew immediately that Elizabeth worked hard the entire day. She did a better job than I think I could've done. She didn't even eat but a few bites of her lunch! I know she gave Sadie the money back, but I want her to have it. She's more than earned it."

Then she looked at me. "Here's the dollar that I owe you for the cleaning, and a dime for the bus, just as I promised."

"Thank you ma'am," I said. "But I don't need the dime. I didn't take the bus. Tommy Viosca gave me a ride home." For the first time, Sadie looked up at me. I could see her out of the corner of my eye, but I just kept looking at her mother. When her mother turned to look at her again, she went back to looking at her shoes.

I hate to admit it, but I smiled inwardly.

"I still think you should have it," she said adamantly. "You should've been able to ride the bus after working so hard; therefore, you still deserve the dime; however, I'm glad that you got a ride home after all. You certainly deserved it after the way my daughter treated you. As a matter of fact, she has something for you, too. Sadie, I think you have something to say?" she said, glaring at her daughter.

Sadie stepped in from behind Mrs. Moore. "Yes ma'am," she said grudgingly. "Beth, I'm sorry for threatening you and saying you hadn't done much work." Her tone said otherwise, and she refused to look at my face again.

Her mother gave her a disapproving look, nudging her. "And?"

Sadie hung her head, thrusting a hand toward me. "Here." It's all she would say, so her mother explained.

"Since Sadie hired you to serve lunch to her friends and spend extra time cleaning up after her, she's also been told she'll pay you for your services. Please, take the money she owes you. I want her to know how much hard work really costs."

I took the money that Sadie had in her hand. I gasped. "This is three and a half dollars!"

"Yes, it is," she said. "I want her to learn her lesson. That's her own money, and I'm making her pay you. It's worth it for her to learn that she can't take advantage of others. Thank you for the work you did, Elizabeth, and I promise to let all my friends know what a great job you do. Mr. and Mrs. Sundo, thank you for letting me talk with your daughter. She seems to be a wonderful girl."

Then Mrs. Moore shook hands with my parents and left. Sadie looked furious, but she wasn't going to say anything negative to her mother.

"Mum, here's the $4.60," I said happily, scarcely able to believe what had just happened.

"Honey, ya earned the money…and the apology," she said. "Why don't ya take a dollar and be done. Go ta the store and get yerself something special. As a matter of fact, take two. Ya deserve it."

"Yes, ma'am!" I said, running upstairs. I hid my money for something I really wanted- a back-to-school dress for fall.

CHAPTER TWENTY

Surprise!

Things seemed to be looking up after that. Mrs. Moore had kept her promise to tell her friends about me, and business was booming. Papa was finding more and more work as well, so money wasn't as tight, and he was a lot more relaxed than he had been in a while.

Even Uncle Elton's job was going better than we expected. We'd been afraid he might lose it when the weather grew warmer and the fires didn't need to be stoked as much, but just the opposite happened. He managed to scare off two would-be burglars one night and became a hero to the bank manager. That got him a raise and secured his job even through the summer months. Papa and I still took turns taking lunch to him every night.

I didn't mind taking lunches to the bank. Whenever I went, I would sit and keep him company while he ate. Sometimes I would try out new recipes for dinner or dessert, and I'd ask for his opinions. I enjoyed spending time with him on those nights.

One evening in particular, I decided to try out a new cake recipe I'd seen in a ladies' magazine. I packed two slices to put into Uncle Elton's lunch and set my alarm for midnight.

When it went off, I got up, heated up his lunch, and headed for the bank. I kept him company while he ate, then we each had a piece of the cake. He loved it.

Afterwards, as I headed home, I grew depressed again. That would have been a great recipe for me to teach to Anna. Thinking about her made me tearful as I rounded the corner and glanced up at my house.

"That's weird," I mumbled aloud when I saw the door was ajar. I couldn't figure out how I'd managed to leave it open. Before I could make it the rest of the way to the house, I saw a man walk up the steps and into the house.

For several moments, I froze. What should I do?

Using all the courage I had, I bolted for the door. I flew up the steps, burst through the door, and came screaming into the house.

"Papa! Papa!" I screamed at the top of my lungs. "There's someone in the house! Papa! Get up!"

"No, Beth, be quiet!" a hushed voice commanded me.

"Papa!" I screamed again, and everything seemed to go nuts.

Papa came running down the stairs with a wooden stick in his hand; Mum was right behind him.

"Who is it?" Papa yelled.

"Beth, be quiet!" the voice commanded again.

"Beth!" Mum was screaming.

Someone let out a scream, and Papa flipped the lights on, and another scream rang out.

"Dale? Is that you?"

I turned and looked. Yes, it was Dale. He stood with a sheepish look.

"Hi," was all he managed to say. Mum ran towards him, throwing her arms around him and, of course, bursting into tears. He picked her up and swirled her around two or three times. By then, Papa and I were running over to hug him, too. He put her down and began to hug us both.

Suddenly, for some reason, I began to beat his chest with my fists.

"Where have you been? Why didn't you tell us you were leaving? Don't you know what you put this family through?"

Mum was drying her tears, and everyone began talking at once.

"Son, where've you been?" Papa asked.

"Have ya eaten?" Typical Mum question.

"I've been working in the south…"

"Doing what?" I asked.

"Heavens, boy, you had us worried," Papa continued.

"Working for the CCC. And no, I haven't eaten, but…"

"Let me get you something ta eat."

"What's the CCC again?"

"Wait a minute! Who's that?" Mum practically shrieked.

The entire room went silent as Papa and I noticed the stranger in the room with us. Standing in the kitchen doorway was a girl, about Dale's age, taller than me but not as tall as Dale. She had beautiful honey-brown hair swept up into the stylish, wavy way that was so popular. We stared.

Quietly, Dale walked over to her and took her hand, then turned to face Mum and Papa.

"We wanted to surprise you in the morning, before breakfast, but here we are. Mum, Papa, Elizabeth, this is Edith Sundo. My wife."

It took a few moments before the enormity of what he'd just said began to sink in. My brother was married? Then the talking to and over each other began all over again.

"What? When?" Mum asked.

"Last Sunday afternoon," Edith said, showing us her new ring.

"Well, congratulations, I think." Papa was so funny.

"Oh, me dears!" Mum exclaimed. She hugged Dale and then Edith, and Papa kissed Edith on the cheek and welcomed her to the family.

"Are you serious? Isn't that wonderful?!" That's all I could say.

Without stopping, everyone moved toward the kitchen to get to know the newest member of our family. Papa started some tea, Mum gathered stuff to make sandwiches, and I started cutting the cake I'd made earlier. Dale and Edith sat at the table and filled us in on everything while we gathered food for our impromptu party.

"So how did you two meet?" Mum asked.

Dale looked Edith in the eyes and took her hand. "Well, you know, I've been working for the CCC," he started, but I interrupted.

"So, what exactly is the CCC again?" I asked, placing the cake plates on the table. "I know it's a government program, but what do the letters stand for? Isn't that part of the army?"

"That's the Civilian Conservation Corps," he explained. "The program is run by the army, but I'm not actually in the army." Then he added the word, "yet."

Mum turned to stare at him.

"Are you thinking about going into the army?" Papa asked.

"I think it's a good possibility," Dale told him. "I really liked working for the CCC."

"Well, that might be good fer ya," Mum said hesitantly. "We'll talk," and she went back to making sandwiches.

"What exactly do they do?" I asked. "The CCC, I mean."

"Well," he began, "Most of the men take care of soil conservation, or they plant trees, or work in national parks. I was working in a national park for a little while, but then I moved to a small park in Texas, and I've been there most of the time. My job was, well, sort of top-secret."

We all held our breath. "Ya aren't doing anything dangerous, are ya?" Mum asked with wide eyes.

Dale laughed. "No, Mum, nothing like that. My job was to take a team into a park at night, and mess it up. We painted graffiti, tore up picnic tables, and threw trash all over the place. I know that sounds strange, but it gave other men a chance to come in and clean up what my team and I'd destroyed earlier. That way, they could earn a paycheck, too." Mum found that amusing.

"Yes, and that's how Dale and I met," said Edith. "My father owns the store where Dale would come in to buy paint. He would paint things and get old cartons to throw around the park. I thought it was kind of strange, but later he told me what he could about his job. Somehow, Dale managed to come in every day to buy paint at about the same time I'd take lunch to my father." Edith blushed and Dale smiled.

"Funny how that just worked out, huh?" he said.

"Oh, that's so sweet," Mum said.

"How did you get to Texas in the first place?" I asked.

Dale chuckled. "Well, that's an interesting story also. See, I got there by train, but I'm afraid I did what we see so many other men doing. I hopped aboard a train and became a hobo."

Dale filled us in on how he'd managed to get from Tennessee to Texas. He'd climbed aboard a train and hung onto the top. There were ladders attached to the top of each car, so he'd lie down on them, wrapping his arms around a rung of the ladder. That way he wouldn't fall off the train while he slept on the trip. It still sounded dangerous to me.

"Honestly, that wasn't always the best idea," he said. "One time, I was on the top of the train when we pulled into a small town in Louisiana. I'd slept through most of the train ride, and I didn't realize I'd been covered in soot and ash from the smoke coming from the engines. Unfortunately, there'd been a bank robbery that same day. The man who robbed the bank apparently had worn black clothes and had black hair. When the police saw me get off the train, they thought I was the bank robber. I was arrested and taken to jail, and that's where they let me take a bath. Once they saw that I wasn't actually wearing black clothes, and my hair was really light brown, they fed me and let me go." He laughed, but Mum was rather upset with him.

"Dale, I don't think that's funny," she scolded. "I'd be ashamed ta have people know that ya were arrested."

"Mum, it's all right," he said. "They know it wasn't me who robbed the bank. Jiminy!"

We talked and laughed all night. Dale told us stories about living in Texas, riding the trains, and about the different people he met. I'd been so angry at him for such a long time, especially since I blamed him for me having to work at the chicken factory. I thought I'd still feel the same way when he got home. Instead, I was so thrilled to have him home I didn't even think about being angry.

The next thing we knew, it was dawn, and Uncle Elton had come home. Mum went to the factory just long enough to let them know that she wouldn't be at work that day. Since I didn't have to clean any kitchens, I was able to stay up as late as I wanted, but finally we all went to bed. I slept for several hours and woke up around noon.

By that time, Mum and Edith were in the kitchen making plans for a special dinner for Saturday evening. I was told that we were to have company. Aunt Martha, Uncle Randall and Dennis would be joining us for a celebration dinner.

I sat down and ate a little bit of late breakfast and drank some tea, but after a while I wandered outside to the front porch. I enjoyed listening to Edith and Mum chatting, but I felt like Mum really wanted to get to know her new daughter-in-law, so I went out to sit on the front porch to read.

After a while, Dale came out on the front steps and sat down beside me. "Hi, Beth."

"Hi."

"So, what do you think of Edith?"

I smiled a genuinely happy smile. "She's wonderful. She's really sweet, and she's awfully pretty."

He grinned. "Thanks. She is pretty special."

"Much too pretty for the likes of you!" I added.

He laughed. "I think Mum likes her, but I think she's worried that we're too young to get married."

"Yeah, I can see that. After all, you're barely 18."

"Yes," he said, sitting up a little straighter. "But I am old enough to go into the army, so I am old enough to get married."

"True."

He got quiet for a moment, then started fiddling around with the laces on his shoes. "Beth, Mum told me you were really angry with me for leaving."

"True," I said, "mostly because Mum and Papa were upset all the time, and because I had to go to work. I hated that factory. I cried at least once a day for the first three months."

"Ouch," he said. "I feel bad enough for leaving. I had no idea it would be so hard on you. I thought I'd go, make some money, send it home, and everyone would be happier, but it took a lot longer than I expected." He was still looking down at his shoes.

"That's all right," I said, and I told him about how we helped the homeless men, and how they all had stories similar to his.

He turned to face me. "Well, again, I'm sorry for everything, especially how you had to go to work." He looked away for a moment. Quietly, he added, "Mum told me about your friend. I'm sorry about that, too."

Tears welled up in my eyes again. I turned and looked down the street so he wouldn't see them. "Yeah. Thank you," was all I could manage.

"How are you handling that? Mum says you are doing all right."

"Everyone thinks I'm all right, and that's what I let them think."

The truth was, on the inside, I was a mess. I had often found myself daydreaming about drastic ways to get revenge on Mr. Reed. I'd be scrubbing a floor and thinking about throwing him off a cliff. Or I'd be putting away dishes and catch myself dreaming up a scenario where he gets run over by one of the company trucks or something.

Fortunately, most of my thoughts were about something less criminal, like sneaking back into the factory to spy on him and Mrs. Fredericks in an effort to prove they were the reason for Anna's death. Or simply walking up to the two of them and telling them I knew the truth. But as always, I set my feelings aside and finished my work.

"I just wish I could prove it," I muttered out loud without realizing it.

"Prove what?" I saw he was staring at me.

"Nothing," I said, a little too swiftly, trying to cover up my thoughts.

"Prove what?" he repeated, a little more forcefully.

I looked him square in the eye. "I think Anna was murdered."

"Murdered?"

I nodded.

"Beth," he said as soothingly as possible, "sometimes, things just happen. I know it hurts, because we want so badly to know why something happens, but sometimes there's just no explanation."

"But Dale," I said, "You don't understand! I know there's more to her dying than we realize. She and I were…"

"Were what?"

I hesitated. It had been kept a secret for so long, but I couldn't share with Anna anymore, and I had to tell someone. "We were finding things out about the boss that was over our department. They were things that Anna wanted to show the factory manager, but she never got the chance."

Dale raised his eyebrows questioningly. For a long time, he and I talked. I told him everything. About how we'd found papers saying that Mrs. Fitzgerald was working in our department, but we'd never actually seen her there; the sign-in sheets showing that there was money set aside for her, but that she never signed saying she received any; how we hadn't even seen her around town to ask her. I even told him about the dream I had where I still thought that Mr. Reed had tried to suffocate me with a pillow.

"That's a strong accusation," he said, "but surely that was just a nightmare from being so sick. I don't think Mum would let a man come into your room while you were sick, or any other time, for that matter."

"I heard Mrs. Fredericks' voice, too," I told him. "I'm just sure they were here. Aunt Martha even said they were! But the worst part is, Dale, one time Mum said that Mr. Reed had done all he could to save Anna. What if he didn't? What if he pushed her?"

He sighed and seemed to be thinking it over. "Well, I don't know how you can prove that," he said, scratching his chin thoughtfully.

"I just want to prove to someone that Mr. Reed was definitely taking money. That'd be enough to show people that I'm not crazy. I'm not just blaming someone out of anger, but that there's reason to believe he pushed her into that grinder."

"Let me think this over," Dale said. "Tell you what. Don't go getting any crazy ideas, all right? Don't do anything stupid, and I'll think about how I can help you."

"Really?" I was shocked.

"Really," he said, giving me a hug. Then he stood up. "I trust you, little sister. But right now, I need to go see my beautiful bride before I head over to Charlie Heckle's Butcher Shop. And I have to stop over at Dr. Viosca's house to see if Tommy and his parents want to join us for dinner tomorrow night, so I need to go."

My stomach lurched. "Tommy's coming here for dinner?"

"Sure, if that's ok with you?" he said in a mocking tone. He knew I had a crush on Tommy. "I want him to meet Edith, and he is my best friend after all."

"I think that'd be a wonderful idea," I told him, standing up to go back into the house. Excitement began to replace the heaviness in my heart.

He opened the door for me and said, "I'll see you in a little while." Then, with a warning glance, he added, "Remember, no crazy ideas, all right?"

I laughingly rolled my eyes. "I understand," I said, disappearing up the stairs. I wanted to pick out a dress and ask my new sister-in-law for advice on my hair.

For one glorious weekend, I would be able to forget about Mr. Reed.

The dinner party that Saturday night turned out to be quite the shindig. I changed dresses three times before Tommy came over, and Edith helped me put my hair into a wavy bun that made me look really grown up.

Everyone came over that night- Aunt Martha, Uncle Randall, Denny, Tommy and his parents, and several of Dale's school friends. Even Uncle Elton got time off from the bank. Everyone brought food to add to the table. It was the biggest feast I think I've ever seen.

Edith charmed everyone, and it was easy to see why. She was as smart and witty as she was pretty. She could tell the funniest jokes, and she told stories of growing up in Texas that were quite hilarious. She told us about her family, their store, and all her friends.

But the thing that really touched everyone's heart was when she overheard Mum say that she wished she could've been at the wedding.

"Why don't we do the wedding over, right now?" Edith offered.

"What?" Dale asked.

"Let's say our vows again so your family can be here. My family was at the last one, so yours can be at this one!"

"That's a wonderful idea!" Aunt Martha said, and everyone else agreed.

Within minutes, we'd decided to set up chairs at the table, Dr. Viosca was our fake priest who would perform the ceremony, and Tommy and I had been asked to be the best man and maid of honor.

We simulated the wedding ceremony, giggling and laughing all the way through because Dr. Viosca couldn't remember the words that were supposed to be said in a wedding, so he made up his own. At one point, he even asked, "Do you, Edith, take this knuckle-headed young-un for your husband? He and my son once spilled paint all over the big tree in my backyard. Are you sure that's what you want?"

"I'm sure," she said, "as long as you tell me that story after the ceremony!" That brought a laugh, too.

Then he asked Dale if he would, "...take this cute tomato for your wedded wife? I think she's too good for you, myself."

"She is, and I definitely do," Dale answered, grinning from ear to ear.

And instead of "You may now kiss the bride," Dr. Viosca ended with, "You may now lay one on her." It was obvious where Tommy got his sense of humor.

After that, we ate and talked and put some records on Aunt Martha's Victrola and danced. At one point, Tommy even took my hand and pulled me up to dance with him. It was midnight before the party ended, and I slept like a rock.

CHAPTER TWENTY-ONE
Reckless Maneuvers

The next few weeks were a jumble of emotions. The party was great, the wedding was great, my work was great, the family was great.

So why did I feel so lousy inside? Maybe it was because my emotions were tied up in knots. I was so happy to have Dale home, and I was happy about his marriage, but I couldn't help but think that Anna should be getting married, too. And now she never would. That part was heartbreaking, but having Tommy ask me to dance was so thrilling that I then felt guilty for having fun. It was like enjoying myself meant I was betraying Anna. Yet, at the same time, I knew she'd be thrilled to find out he'd asked me to dance.

Having so many emotions going in so many different directions had my nerves set on edge. I was jumpy and couldn't explain why. I couldn't concentrate while I was working because I had all that time to ponder while I was scrubbing floors. It was even worse at night. It all invaded my dreams, making sleep difficult.

There was a storm that night; the night I went back to the factory. It was a Tuesday night- actually, I guess it was early Wednesday morning. I was having a really hard time sleeping. I felt like I was constantly in that state of sleep where you aren't asleep yet, but you aren't actually awake, either. Then I'd have a dream and wake up just enough to know it was a dream, and not be able to sleep peacefully.

I'm not sure what the last dream was, but when the lightning struck, I bolted straight up in the bed, consumed with rage. My fists were clenched; hot tears were streaming down my face. I was infuriated, and my heart was pounding so loud it seemed it could wake up Mum and Papa down the hallway.

It was several minutes before I could get my heartbeat to slow down enough to relax. I was finally able to lie back down, but my mind kept battling back and forth.

Downstairs, I heard Dale returning from visiting with Uncle Elton. Since Mum, Papa, and I all had work the next day, he'd offered to take lunch to the bank. After a few moments, the house grew silent again.

Yet my thoughts stirred.

One thing seemed to lead to another. The mere idea of sleep was gone, so I got dressed. And as long as I was getting dressed, I went ahead and put on my shoes and socks. I didn't feel like reading or sewing, so I went downstairs. Staring out the window, I kept wondering why Anna hadn't left me a message the day of her accident saying she was going to go ahead and confront Mr. Reed.

Suddenly, my mind began to race.

What if she had? What if Anna had written me a message and just didn't have time to get it to Mum? Would she have left it where I could find it?

No, I decided dejectedly. There was no way she would have known she was going to die. Besides, that was four months ago. Anything she left would have been found and destroyed by now.

The clock said it was a little after three, and the rain had subsided, so I wandered out to the front porch to sit on one of the rocking chairs Mum kept out there. I sat down for maybe two minutes when I realized I was too restless to sit anywhere. I had to get up and move around.

The rain was gone, leaving the streets quiet and glistening. I slipped off the porch and started walking. Before I knew it, I was running. It was like some invisible force was pushing me there. I had to be there. I had to see where Anna died. I had to do... well, *something*.

The air, chilled by the summer rains, cooled me off as I ran. I didn't care that my old dress was getting muddy; I just ran. I didn't want anyone to see me. I wanted to be alone.

There was once that I thought I heard someone call my name. I was afraid it was Dale, and perhaps he'd seen me leave, so I hid behind a trash can for a few moments. Fortunately, I didn't hear anything else except for a car passing by my hiding place. After it was gone, I snuck back out and went towards the factory once again.

When I approached the fence, I slowed down. For the longest time, I just stood there, staring at it; hating it and everything in it.

Then I remembered the hole. People kept saying someone should fix this large hole in the fence, but no one really seemed to care about it. I didn't know if I could find it in the dark, but I tried anyway. And there it was.

Carefully, I pulled the wire away from the fence and eased through it. It caught a piece of my dress, and I could hear it tearing. Pulling the fabric away, I freed myself and continued to the loading docks in the back of the factory.

Standing on the cold, dark, wet grass, I stared at it for a while. There just had to be some clue Anna had left for me. I thought perhaps, if I found it and showed it to Mum, she could take it to the owner of the plant; then Mr. Reed and Mrs. Fredericks would have to pay for what they'd done, and...

Someone called out and made me almost jump out of my skin. There were people at the plant already! I ran and hid behind an old, broken down truck that smelled of gasoline. When all was quiet again, I ran around to get closer to the trucks in the dock, preparing for the daily deliveries.

There weren't any drivers in sight, so I darted across to the stairs to the door leading into the top part of the loading docks. The back door had been left ajar, so I pulled it back and peered in. Since the coast seemed to be clear, I tip-toed in and started to walk into the warehouse.

That's when I saw it. I was standing in front of it.

On my right I saw the gigantic wheels and sharp blades of the box grinder that cut up empty, unusable boxes. I was staring at the very piece of equipment that took Anna's life and crumpled it up into death.

And on my left, I could see the hallway that led to the supervisors' offices. To Mr. Reed's office.

Tears warmed my cheeks as my mind envisioned the scene that must have been Anna's last few minutes. In my mind, I could hear the screaming and chaos, and I couldn't even handle the horror of how much agony she must have endured with those sharp blades and crushing pain of giant wheels.

There was no way I could stare at it any longer, so I ran down the hallway leaving a trail of my tears along the way, because I knew. I knew she'd been there. I knew she'd either been caught by him, or was confronting him, because there was no other reason for her to have passed his office to get to the loading docks. There was no other reason she would even have been in that part of the factory.

For some reason, I ran to the locker rooms to sit down and cry. The main part of the plant still wasn't open yet, so I knew I was safe. No one would see me. I let the heaving sobs take over until I could breathe normally again.

I have no idea how long I was there, but when I got up, I started to look for clues in Anna's locker. But there was someone else's lock on it, reminding me that the locker now belonged to whoever had replaced Anna.

With a sinking heart, I gave up on the idea of finding any clues. Everything would be locked up, and there was no way I could wait around for Mrs. Fredericks to open her door unless I hid in the bathroom stalls until all the other workers arrived. And that idea was ridiculous.

It was in that moment I realized I hadn't thought this plan through at all. It was time to return home. I had to be ready to go clean someone's kitchen in a few hours and needed to get some rest.

As I made my way through the dark halls, away from the loading docks, I absentmindedly grabbed the knob on Mrs. Fredericks' office door, and much to my surprise, it turned!

In a state of shock, I looked around. No one was there. It was silent. There was no light coming out from under the door.

It was too good to be true. I tuned the knob again and pushed the door open and stepped inside.

It was my only chance.

Quickly I turned on the lamp, and rifled through papers on her desk, looking for Mrs. Fitzgerald's name again, but I didn't see it. I went over to the filing cabinet to see if there were any more papers hidden behind it, but again I thought how the months had passed. Mrs. Fredericks had certainly cleaned behind it by now. Hoping beyond hope that I would find another paper using Mrs. Fitzgerald's name, I opened the filing cabinet and started looking through the file of signature sheets. I thumbed through them, but I didn't see her name appear on any sign-in sheets. I grabbed a couple of older ones, and I took them out of the cabinet completely. I desperately thumbed through those as well.

These were the older ones, and I knew because I saw my name.

I remembered Mrs. Fitzgerald's name and mine had been on the same page. I saw my name again, but not hers. Then I realized, to my amusement, that of course it wouldn't be here. It was the wrong department. And the wrong date.

I breathed in sharply. My name?

I looked again. Yes, there was my name saying I received my pay, but that wasn't my signature. It also wasn't my department. This was the canning department. In May. But I hadn't been there since the day I got sick *in February*.

I trembled as my mind began to fully realize what I was holding. I had it.

I had the proof!

Although I'd not been there once since February, I held at least five pages saying that I'd been receiving my full wages from the canning department for the last five weeks. Mr. Reed, and most likely Mrs. Fredericks as well, had made it look like I'd just taken a transfer to a different department after Anna's death, and was therefore still getting paid. They must be keeping the extra money!

My vision went blurry; I wasn't sure if they were tears of joy, relief, or sorrow, but a couple began to make their way down my cheeks and fall onto the papers.

"We've got them, Anna! I have the proof," I whispered to the empty room.

I spun around and quickly turned off the lamp on her desk. Hurrying, I made my way out of the office and down the hall. I was so proud of myself, and all I'd have to do was to take these papers to my mum, then she could give them to the police. I might not be able to see him in jail for Anna's murder, I decided, but I could certainly get him there for embezzling money from the company!

I made my way down the hall, thrilled to have my treasure in my hands. Maybe that's why I wasn't paying attention.

I'd decided to go back out of the factory grounds the way I'd come in: through the hole in the fence. I was so excited that I was almost running as I headed towards Mr. Reed's office. I came to a screeching halt as I heard his door open.

I practically dove behind some boxes, barely making it before I saw him pass me. I held my breath as he passed by me, close enough I could've touched him. Worse, he could've reached over and grabbed me, but he just kept going.

I finally exhaled. Making sure that no one else was around, I snuck out of my hiding place. I was going to leave, but he'd left his door open. I just had to know.

I walked in.

It was the same office I'd been brought to on the first day he hired me all those months ago. It was dull and drab, just like I remembered. Small, dirty, and barely furnished. The single desk was covered in a few papers, a couple of pencils, and a letter opener or two. Other than that, there was only a chair, a filing cabinet, and the clock on it that reminded me that the sun would be rising soon. It was almost summer, after all.

I had to hurry.

Brushing past the chair, I laid down the papers I'd been carrying on the seat. I began searching his desk, but found nothing, so I had to look in the filing cabinet. I had no idea what I was looking for, but I had to look. Maybe I'd find something that would help me; I just had to!

I searched and searched for a clue, but found nothing.

"Hey, what're you-" I heard a voice behind me say. I almost had a heart attack as I turned around.

"Beth Sundo? What're you doing here?" Mr. Reed demanded.

"I, uh. I just, uh..." There was nothing to say at first. But as I stared at his face, the anger and the hatred came rushing forward. A year's worth of emotion spewed forth like steam from a tea kettle.

"You killed her, didn't you?" I accused.

His face paled as he narrowed his eyes. "I don't know what you're talking about," he said coldly. "But you have no right to be here. Get out before I call the police on you."

How dare he! My fury and pain rose higher. "You did! I know you did! You killed her! You pushed Anna into the grinder! Murderer!" My voice grew shrill, breaking as tears of anger gathered in my eyes. Mr. Reed's face grew a mottled purple suddenly.

"It was an accident!" he yelled back, stepping toward me. "I just pushed her, to make her shut up, and she fell. It was your fault anyway!" He was waving his finger in my face.

"My fault?! How was it my fault?!"

"You two brats should've left everything alone. I wouldn't have pushed her, but she was yelling at me! Now you're doing the same thing! I'm warning you...."

I couldn't stop.

"Accident? You tried to kill me, too, didn't you? But that was no accident. When I was at home, sick, in my own bed! You tried to kill me there, didn't you? DIDN'T YOU?!"

He suddenly grabbed me by the collar of my dress. "I should've!" His eyes shown with fury, as his voice dropped. "You just can't shut up, can you?" he said, his voice growing icy, as he clenched the collar with both hands and started pushing me toward the back of the office. "I guess I'll have to shut you up myself!"

He pushed again and let go of me just long enough to reach for one of the letter openers on his desk. Desperately, I pushed against him so he couldn't reach it. He spun me around to where my back was to him and went for the opener again. I wanted to hit him, and hit him hard. I shoved my elbow into his sizable round stomach with as much force as I could muster and heard him grunt out "Oof!" and he let go.

Everything after that happened so quickly. I tried to run for the door, but the chair was in my way. He grabbed my arm. I turned, raking my nails down his arm, and he grunted with pain, but didn't let go. I kicked and kicked. In the struggle, I felt the pain of him landing a punch on my cheek.

"Stop it, you little brat!" he yelled, trying to catch my other arm.

"No!" I squealed. "Leave me alone!"

I scratched his face, and he grabbed my wrists.

"You want to see how she died? I can show you!" he snarled.

I threw my legs up as he tried to push me through the open doorway, bracing myself against the door frame with all my might. It was just enough to throw him off balance. He let go of me to catch himself. I wanted to get out, but I had to have those papers first. I ran and threw my entire weight into his stomach with my shoulder, knocking him to the side. I practically bounced off of him and hit the floor, knocking the stack of papers off of the chair.

"No!" I screamed. I grabbed as many papers as I could and ran for the door.

Mr. Reed had been knocked back into the wall, next to the filing cabinet, and was regaining his balance. He darted toward me, catching me by the arm, which spun me around, toward the filing cabinet. I let go of the papers and wriggled my hand loose. Grabbing the thick, heavy clock from the top of the filing cabinet, I swung it at the side of his head. It connected to the side of his face, and with a loud thud, he hit the floor.

I grabbed up as many of the papers as I could and sprinted for the door again. For a fat man, he got up pretty quickly and woozily grabbed at my arm. As his fingers clutched at me, my sleeve tore, and I was free, leaving the material clasped in his fist.

Wordlessly, I screamed, and got out of the door and down the hallway.

Two men were running towards us. I pushed past them and kept running. I supposed they were too shocked to grab me.

"Boss, what's wrong?" one of the men called out, still running toward Mr. Reed. "We heard yelling!"

"Get her!" he yelled as he made his way through the door, still clutching his head. "She's stealing from the company!"

I heard the men turn and start towards me about the time I hit the door to the loading docks. Now there were three men chasing me. I was almost hysterical as I ran and took a full leap off the side of the loading dock and landed on the rocky ground that made up the driveway. My feet slipped on the gravel and I almost fell but caught myself with my hand. I turned around, and they were behind me, but they were taking the stairs down to the lower level.

I kept running. I ran past the weeds and down to the hole in the fence that I'd used getting into the plant.

"Beth! Beth!" a man's voice was yelling, but I wasn't about to stop. I slid through the hole in the fence, slicing my bare arm along the way, but I didn't really notice.

I looked back, and there were men still following me. I kept running, and they kept calling my name.

Then out of nowhere, two men appeared on my side of the fence and grabbed me. I struggled and screamed, but no matter what I did, I couldn't get free.

"Stop it! Stop it!" I screamed. I jerked back and forth, shoving their hands away, but they were far stronger than me. I bit, I scratched, I screamed, but to no avail. They managed to get me into a waiting car. One held me down and the other one started driving.

I fought like a wild thing, but his strong hands held me in the back seat of the car. After I managed to kick him in the shins, he pushed me down onto the seat, and I felt the sharp sting of pain as he slapped me across the face.

I stared into his face; I gasped.

I couldn't believe he hit me!

And then, I suppose I must have passed out.

CHAPTER TWENTY-TWO

Truth and Consequences

I opened my eyes, and it took me a minute to realize where I was and who I was with. I stared at him.

"Dale?"

Dale glared at me. His words were cold and choppy. "Yeah, it's me. Are you ok now?"

"You hit me!"

"Yeah, sorry about that," he said, still looking a bit frustrated. "You were hysterical. I kept telling you that it was me, but you kept fighting me and, well, little sister, you are stronger than you look. You were hurting me!"

I sat up in the back of the car. "Oh. I'm sorry." We sat there silently for a moment, and I burst into tears.

"What happened to Mr. Reed?" I asked him.

"I think we outsmarted him," The man in the front seat said. "We got you before he did and put you in the car. Did he hurt you?"

I was stunned. The man in the front seat was Tommy! "No, no, I'm fine," I said, trying to sound brave, but I knew my voice quivered and gave it away.

"Are you sure you're ok? You look sort of beat up."

I looked at my hands and dress and legs for the first time. He was right. I did look as if I'd been beaten. My hands were scraped and bleeding from where I had skidded on the gravel. My muddied dress was torn, my bare arm was bleeding, and my legs were scratched up. "Yes, I don't suppose I look very pleasant," I mumbled.

"Wait till you see the black eye," Dale said. "I hope the other guy looks as bad!"

"Black eye?" I moaned.

"Yes," Dale said. "Elizabeth Anne Sundo, what on earth were you thinking?"

I peeked into the rearview mirror and gingerly touched the raising bruise under my eye. "I was just trying to get some proof that Mr. Reed killed Anna."

Dale rolled his eyes. "Beth, you can't..."

"Oh, but I can!" I fussed at him. "He admitted it! He told me he pushed her because she was screaming at him. They got into a fight, and he pushed her! He told me!"

"Calm down, calm down," Dale said. I took a deep breath.

"Well, can they prove that in court?" Tommy said as he drove around the corner.

"I don't know, but I can prove he was stealing from the company!" I retorted. Then I gasped. "Where are those papers? Where are the papers I had in my hand?" They were gone. I felt my eyes well up. It had all been for nothing.

"You mean these?" Tommy said, holding them up from his seat in the front of the car.

A wave of relief swept over me. "Oh, Tommy! You found them! Thank you so much."

"What are they?" Dale asked as I grabbed them from Tommy.

"Look at these," I told Dale.

Tommy pulled into a parking space in front of a store, stopped the car, and turned around to listen. In the morning light, I was able to show them to him. "I have papers that prove he was taking money for workers who were not even working at the factory."

"And how can you prove this?" Dale asked.

"See? Right here. He has me down on a list of people who signed this ledger saying that we got paid. I never got paid, because I haven't been paid since I left back in February, and that is certainly not my handwriting. Someone else signed my name, and I know Mr. Reed knew all about it. I know he did because Mum told him I quit. She didn't want me there after Anna died."

"Well, I'll be," Dale muttered. "And look at the dates. You're right. I think we need to go to the police station and show this to someone down there."

"The police station?" I wasn't sure what to think, although that'd been my original plan as well.

"So is that where we're headed next?" Tommy asked, looking only at Dale.

"Yes, I think it's best," he said. Tommy turned around and started the engine of the car again. I looked through the back window to see if Mr. Reed had followed us, but I didn't see him.

I had a sudden thought. "Dale, how'd you know to come and get me?"

He gave me a sharp look. "I didn't. You need to thank Tommy. He came and got me at the house this morning."

"You did?" I asked.

Tommy turned his head and winked.

"I wasn't really trying to 'save' you," he explained. "It just kind of… happened. I was coming back from dropping my father off at the McDouglas house- Mrs. McDouglas is going to have her baby any time now- and I thought I saw you walking along the street. I drove by again, but I couldn't find you. I thought perhaps you were coming to get my father for something, so I ran by your house to see if someone was sick. Fortunately, Dale answered the door. When we realized you weren't in your room, he figured out where you were going."

I thought about it for a moment and chuckled. "You must've been in the car I heard passing by when I was hiding behind the trash cans."

He looked amused. "I called your name several times, but you never answered me. I wasn't even sure it was you after a while. That's why I went to your house, just in case."

"Sure it is," Dale chided. I wasn't sure what that meant, so I just looked at him. He winked at me and silently mouthed, "He likes you!"

My heart almost stopped beating in my chest. I turned to look at Tommy, who was still chatting about how they found me.

"Then we saw you coming out of the area by the fence. I saw those men chasing you, but—good grief—you're a fast little girl. If you hadn't been in danger, I would have laughed at those old, fat men trying to keep up with you!"

We pulled into the front of the police station, and Dale started to get out of the car. I couldn't move. "Dale, maybe we shouldn't."

"Oh, no," he said. "You went to all of this trouble, and you found true proof that this Reed person was stealing, so we're going. Besides, I want them to see how he beat you up."

"But Mum and Papa can take care of that," I pleaded.

"No way," he said, half laughing and half serious. "If we take you home looking like this, Papa will go and kill him. I'd much prefer to see Reed in jail instead of Papa, thank you. But I'll tell you what. I'll send Tommy to go get them for you, all right?"

"Sure!" Tommy interjected. "I'll go get them *and* let them know you're safe, OK?"

I still didn't want to go, but in a way, Dale had a point, and I'd planned to go with Mum to the police station anyhow. Reluctantly, I looked at that large, red-bricked building in front of me and slid out of the car. Dale followed, shut the door, and gave Tommy some instructions.

"Just be gentle when you tell them about how she looks. I don't want my parents to go crazy and hurt someone."

"I don't have to mention that at all, if you don't want me to."

"I think you should," Dale told him. "I don't want them to be shocked, either. That might send Papa into a rage as well."

Tommy nodded, and he waved as he put the car in motion. We turned and walked through the front doors.

Three police officers came walking up to us when they saw me walk in. Each one of them asked if we were all right. I stood quietly by, holding the papers in my hand, while Dale explained everything to them.

After he finished, one of the officers sternly said, "Wait here. I'll get the sergeant."

Dale put his arm around me. "It'll be all right. I'll stay with you while we sort this thing out."

For the first time in a while, I felt safe. There were police officers all around me, each one of them armed. I knew there was no way Mr. Reed could get to me now.

The sergeant finally came out of an office. "You must be Miss Sundo," he said.

I nodded.

With a gentle smile, he put his hand out to shake mine. "I'm Sergeant Anderson. What do you say we talk in my office?"

I nodded again, and I turned to look at Dale.

"I promise not to leave until you're done," he said. "And Mum and Papa should be here by the time you're finished."

"All right," I said, and I followed the sergeant into the office.

I know I was in that office for at least two hours. There were people writing down everything I said, some lady came and took pictures of my injuries, and I had to write out what happened on a piece of paper. When I finally came out, Mum and Papa were waiting outside in the hallway. I saw my mum, and I ran into her arms.

"Mum, I'm so sorry," I started. "I just had to go to the factory. I was sure Anna'd left me a note or something. I'm so sorry I went back, but I had to. And now you're missing work because of me!"

Mum cupped my face in her hands. "'Tis fine," she said. "They closed the factory when the police showed up. I'm not missing any work. And we'll get through this. Tommy and yer brother told us everything. I'm sorry I didn't realize how cruel Mr. Reed and Mrs. Fredericks had been ta ya. If I had…"

"They're just lucky the police got to them before I did," Papa said, touching his fingers to my aching black eye.

"The police already have them?" I asked. "Did they pick them up at the factory?"

"Well, they have Mrs. Fredericks," Mum told me. "I saw them bring her in fer questioning."

"Mr. Reed is still out there," Papa added. "He apparently ran from the factory when he realized you were gone with those… whatever those papers are that everyone keeps talking about."

"I gave those to the sergeant," I told him.

"Mr. and Mrs. Sundo, could I have a word with you in my office?" Sergeant Anderson asked.

"All right," Mum said. "Ya stay here with Dale, and we'll be back."

"Yes, ma'am," I said. Papa hugged me and kissed me on the forehead. "I'm still a little mad about you putting yourself in such danger, but I'm proud of you. If this man is the monster I think he is, he'd better turn himself in before I get to him."

With that, Mum and Papa left to go talk to the police officers. I sat on the bench, and my brother sat beside me.

"Where's Edith?" I asked.

"Mum said she's at home, cooking up breakfast and letting Aunt Martha and Uncle Randall know what's going on, and cancelling your house-cleaning appointment for you."

I sighed. "Good. I'd forgotten all about that."

We sat in silence for a few more minutes.

"Dale, I know what I did was dumb, but do you think it'll help at all?"

Dale shrugged and leaned up against the wall. He looked drained. "I can't guarantee anything, but I'm pretty sure it will. After all, perhaps you're saving the company some money, and that can't hurt. Besides, if Mr. Reed and that Mrs. Fredericks lady are fired, which I'm pretty sure they will be, then maybe you made it easier on some other workers. Like Mum, for instance. Or another girl like you that doesn't deserve to be treated the way you were treated. All in all, I think you did a good thing."

I smiled and leaned against the wall as well. "Thanks."

Then suddenly, he wrapped his big arm my neck and used his other hand to knuckle-rub my head. "And if you ever do anything like this to me or Mum or Papa again, I'm going to give you a black eye myself! Do you get me, Little Sister?"

I laughed. "All right, all right! I promise!" I gasped between the giggles.

And at the same time, I thought, "I hope you can see this, Anna!"

Independence Day

July Fourth turned out to be a warm day, but the breezes were cool. The band was playing the national anthem while a well-dressed woman sang the words. Before I knew it, I was singing aloud with her, then the crowd around me joined in as well. It seemed especially beautiful to me right then. I'm not sure why.

It was an almost perfect day, and I was wishing I had someone to share it with besides my family. Mum and Papa were there, and so were Dale and Edith. Even Uncle Elton was there with a date. He'd started courting a lady he met at the market. Everyone seemed to have someone special to share the day with except me.

Maybe the real reason I was feeling so alone was because, during the last Fourth of July Picnic, I'd spent the day talking with my best friend in the world, and now she wasn't there to enjoy this glorious day.

Suddenly, someone grabbed my arm. I spun around and yanked my arm away, then realized it was Tommy.

"Sorry!" he said, releasing me immediately. "I'm so sorry. I didn't mean to startle you."

"It's all right," I said, laughing. "I just thought it might be Mr. Reed."

"Really? Are you still scared of him? He's still in jail, you know."

"Yes, I know. I guess I'm just afraid he'll get out or something and come after me, you know? Like in the movies?"

"Yes, I heard he tried to escape once," he said, looking around like he was trying to catch Mr. Reed stalking us. "But even if he did escape, I don't think he'd come after you. I think he'd try to leave town instead. He knows he's going to be found guilty and just doesn't want to serve his jail time. That's all."

"Yeah, I was told that, too. I guess I'm just jumpy."

"I can understand why. The trial starts Monday, right?"

I nodded.

"You still going to testify?"

"Yes, I am."

A low whistle came from his lips. "I think that makes you one of the bravest people I know. I don't know many girls who would testify in court about a man they're afraid of. I'm not sure I would, and I'm a man."

Then he grinned. "Well, almost a man, anyway. I'm starting college this fall. I'm going to be a doctor, just like my father."

"Really? That's wonderful. Another doctor! So, where will you go to school?"

"Here in Pittsburgh," he said, looking rather proud of himself. "Well, at least that's where I'll start. I will probably have to go to Philadelphia for some part of my training, but that won't be for a while yet."

"Oh, so that means you'll still be here in town. That's delightful. And I'll be going back to school this fall, too."

"Oh, Beth, that's terrific. I know you've been wanting this for a while."

"I sure have," I answered. "With Mum, Papa, and Uncle Elton all working, and Dale going into the military, Mum said we could afford for me to not work anymore, so I can go to school. I've already talked to my friend, Allison, and she's ready for me to come back as well."

"That's swell," he said.

There was a moment of silence between us. Finally, he said, "Would you like to go to the contest tents with me? My mom entered a pie baking contest, and I want to see how she did."

"Oh, yes!" I said, looking at my watch. "That'd be lovely. I wanted to go see how Edith did in the sewing contest as well."

"All right," he said, offering me his arm. I wasn't sure what to do, so I slowly put my arm through his, and he began to lead the way to the tents.

"Oh, wait!" he said suddenly. "What about your house-cleaning business? Won't you have to give it up?"

I shrugged. "I don't mind. I can always do it on a Saturday if I need to earn a little extra money. But to tell the truth, my Aunt Martha said I could come help her out at her store if I want. I think I'd like that. She lets me get stuff at a cheaper price, and I can help her make cookies and pies for the less fortunate. I like that idea, too."

He smiled. "That sounds like a good job for you."

"It is," I agreed, just as we passed some picnic tables.

I looked over and saw a group of girls giggling as some boys were arm wrestling. I caught a glimpse of Sadie as she was "ooh-ing" and "aah-ing" over the boy winning the match.

"Would you like to go over there?" I asked hesitantly. I didn't really want to go, but they looked like Tommy's friends, so I thought I'd be polite.

To my surprise, Tommy rolled his eyes. "No, not really. Sadie Moore's over there. Do you know Sadie?"

I didn't exactly lie, but I didn't tell him the entire truth, either. "I know who she is, but we're not friends or anything."

He sort of glared in her direction. "She's such a flirt. I had to drive her to my house once, just to get my father's doctor bag, and she started acting as if we were courting. That was one of the longest drives of my life! She's just so obvious."

This time, I chuckled, because I remembered the day I saw them in the car together, and I thought about how Anna'd said the same thing about her.

Anna. My heart dropped a beat. I missed Anna.

"Are you ok?" Tommy asked suddenly. "You look really sad."

I was sad. And I was happy at the same time. Anna was right; Tommy could see right through Sadie and her atrocious ways. "I'm fine. I was just thinking of something Anna said once."

Tommy looked a little sad, too. "I'm so sorry you had to go through that. But thanks to you, Mr. Reed is going to jail. What did they decide to do to that lady that was helping him?"

I rolled my eyes. "Mrs. Fredericks, you mean? Well, she admitted to seeing Mr. Reed push Anna into that machine. It was partly an accident, but it was still his fault. So, she confessed that she'd been helping him steal money, and she only has to be in jail for six months if she tells them the truth in court."

"Good grief!" was all Tommy said.

"That worked out for us," I shrugged. "My mum was able to take over her job as line foreman, and now she's making more money. That's part of the reason I can go back to school now."

"That's such good news," he said, and he squeezed my hand.

"Yoo-hoo, Tommy!" Sadie called over to us. "Hello!"

"Hi," Tommy called as he waved, a fake smile covering his face. I waved, too.

I saw the look on Sadie's face when she realized he was holding my hand in his. She went red and her eyes were wide. I hadn't realized she was so self-absorbed that she hadn't even noticed I was there until after she had already called out to him.

Tommy bent down toward my ear. "Let's leave here before she comes over," he said quietly.

"Absolutely!" It was fine with me.

As he swept us away from the picnic tables and toward the tents, I looked over my shoulder. Sadie just stared after us. I don't usually take delight in someone else's misfortune, but it was nice having her be jealous of me for once.

Tommy cleared his throat. "Would you mind if I were to ask your father if I may give you a ride home after the fireworks tonight?"

I couldn't help but burst into a huge smile. "I'd like that."

He looked relieved. "That's great," he told me.

We walked along in silence for a moment, my beau and me.

"So," he ventured, "tell me about the trial. Do you know what you are going to say?"

"Well, sort of," I told him. "The lawyer prepared me for the questions I'll be asked."

"Like what?"

"Well, like… like how did Anna and I know about the fake names on the pay sheets, and when did we suspect about the money? Why was I in the office at three in the morning? And how did you and Dale just happen to know where I was? It's like they want me to tell them the whole story, but I think that's impossible."

"Why?" he asked.

"Well, it's hard to say when it started. That could be when the stock market crashed, or when Papa lost his job and Mum had to go to work. But I think the real story started the day my mum came home and said she had some 'Great News' for me."

Thank you to the Financial Backers of my Kickstarter Campaign...

S. Brooke Chavez
Jana Christian
Donna "DC" Clark
Jason Culotta
Teresa D'Onfro
Heather Gingrich
Linda Hensel
Shelley Hudson
Jennifer Jordan
Tom Jordan
Leda Juengerman
J. J. R. Lewald
Carey Lotzer
Jenny Maddox
Kevin and Janett O'Brien
Margaret O'Brien
David and Kelly Patterson
Ciara Pena
Jennifer Purkey
Misty Williams Rangel
Kay Reid
Leigh Reid
Ainslie Robinson
Michael Spencer
Danny and Sherrie Stanley
Frank and Dawn Stone
Paul and Jean Storm
Pat and Rose Thomas
Ellen Tillman
Monte and Laura Warren
Rick and Candace Walkley

www.ingramcontent.com/pod-product-compliance
Lightning Source LLC
LaVergne TN
LVHW021700060526
838200LV00050B/2431